The
Dechronization
of
Sam Magruder

Introduction
by Arthur C. Clarke

Afterword
by Stephen Jay Gould

Edited and with a memoir
by Joan Simpson Burns

St. Martin's Press
New York

The Dechronization of Sam Magruder

A Novel by

George

Gaylord

Simpson

INTRODUCTION copyright © 1996 by Arthur C. Clarke

AFTERWORD copyright © 1996 by Stephen Jay Gould

ILLUSTRATIONS copyright © 1996 by Richard Roe
Design by Pei Loi Koay

Library of Congress Cataloging-in-Publication Data

Simpson, George Gaylord, 1902–1984
    The dechronization of Sam Magruder : a novel / by George Gaylord Simpson ; intro. by Arthur C. Clarke ; afterword by Stephen Jay Gould : a brief commentary about the work by Joan Simpson Burns.
        p.   cm.
    ISBN 0-312-13963-2
    1. Time travel—Fiction.   I. Title.
PS3537.I743D43   1996
813'.54—dc20   95-36146
                                                            CIP

First Edition: January 1996

10   9   8   7   6   5   4   3   2   1

Contents

Introduction

The Exploration of Time

by Arthur C. Clarke

It's Saturday, 15 January 1994, and I'm trying to cope with the usual bomb-load of mail, made worse by the fact that yesterday was a holiday—Thai Pongal, the Hindu New Year. Two items are of particular, and closely related, interest, though their origins are completely different.

First is a letter from my friend Dr. Charles Pellegrino, the scientist who suggested the idea behind *Jurassic Park*—i.e., that it might be possible to clone dinosaurs from DNA obtained from bloodsucking insects preserved in amber. Charlie's letter includes a Gary Larson "Far Side" cartoon, which shows a parking lot full of cars, interspersed with a handful (if that's the right word) of dinosaurs. Yes, you've guessed its title. . . .

Well, in the very same mail as Charlie's letter I receive a notice from the H. G. Wells Society announcing that in July 1995 there will be an international symposium at H.G.'s alma mater, the Kensington Imperial

College of Science and Technology, to mark the centenary of *The Time Machine*—and asking me if I could give the keynote address. Alas, the days are long gone when I regularly commuted from Sri Lanka to the West, and I had just composed my letter of regrets when the postman arrived with a special delivery package.

Inside was a slim typescript bearing a rather forbidding title, *The Dechronization of Sam Magruder*. It was the third manuscript to arrive in the last twenty-four hours, and I automatically reached for the form letter which I have been sending out for years, explaining why I can no longer read unsolicited manuscripts.

Then I noticed the author's name on the title page and did a double take. The cover letter, from Joan Simpson Burns, explained everything:

> Dear Dr. Clarke,
> I am enclosing a copy of a short time-travel fiction written by my father, the late evolutionist George Gaylord Simpson, as well as copies of two letters from Stephen Jay Gould. We would be extravagantly pleased if you would be willing to write an accompanying piece . . . to precede the novella. . . . Professor Gould has agreed to write an afterword and would be delighted to have you join our project. . . .

Knowing the reputations of both Simpson and Gould, I was, of course, flattered by the proposal—but also embarrassed. I was already involved in several major projects, so how to decline as gracefully as possible? However, I'd certainly have a look at the manuscript . . . it wasn't too long—about 25,000 words. . . .

I started reading, and was immediately hooked. Professor Simpson had—deliberately, I am sure—used exactly the same format as Wells. His speakers bore not names but labels: the Universal Historian, the Pragmatist, the Ethnologist, the Common Man (*vide* Wells's the Medical Man, the Provincial Mayor, the Editor—and, of course, the Time Traveller). Yet in some respects Simpson had gone much beyond H.G., who needed only a contemporary 1895 setting to frame his story. Because no one has yet, at least up to the latest CNN bulletin, invented a time machine, Simpson had to set his tale well into *our* future, and makes it clear by subtle hints that it is very different from the present world, often in unexpected ways.

The more I read, the more I was impressed—and moved—by the ordeals, triumphs, and ultimate fate of Simpson's indomitable hero, and once again I was reminded of the magical epilogue of *The Time Machine*:

> It may be that he swept back into the past . . . into the abysses of the Cretaceous Sea; or among the grotesque saurians, the huge reptilian brutes of the Jurassic times. He may even now—if I may use the phrase—be wandering on some plesiosaurus-haunted Oolithic coral reef, or beside the lonely saline lakes of the Triassic Age.

"*Even now!*" The paradoxical implications of that phrase have haunted me ever since I first encountered it, at least half a century ago. It was obvious that there was more than a trace of wish fulfillment in Simpson's fantasy—indeed, can any paleontologist have failed to have dreamed of traveling into the past?

By yet another coincidence, I had just sent my agent, Russell Galen, a tongue-in-cheek fax threatening that *my* next project would be called "Triassic Zoo": and when Simpson's manuscript arrived, I realized that my little joke had backfired. I *really* would have to become involved with dinosaurs again, whether I liked it or not. They had, after all, been responsible for triggering my own interest in science. . . .

I can still recall the incident, nearly seventy years ago, when my father handed me a cigarette card while we were riding together in a small two-wheeled cart drawn by one of our farm ponies. Unless my imagination has created a retrospective image, I can still see the exact spot where this happened.

The card showed a picture of a most extraordinary animal—a kind of lizard, with a huge spiky fan erected along its back. It was, I read, a *Stegosaurus*, and I treasured that card for a long time, using it as inspiration for little tales I recounted to a captive—and probably restive—audience of classmates in my village school. The fact that I remember this incident so vividly, after such a lapse of time, proves how important it was in my mental development.

For several years, paleontology was one of my chief

interests; I collected fossils and haunted the local museum. Then I suddenly switched to astronomy, for reasons I can no longer recall. Dinosaurs were superseded by spaceships, but I still possess a remarkable series of black-and-white stereo photographs issued as cigarette cards. Though they must have been made in the 1920s, they are absolutely convincing—as good as the stills from *Jurassic Park* itself. There is no sense of scale, and I have often wondered just how large the models were, and what now-forgotten genius created them. They would have fully merited the compliment one film reviewer paid to *Jurassic Park*: "You can't tell the real dinosaurs from the fake ones."

Perhaps the project was inspired by the film version of Arthur Conan Doyle's classic, *The Lost World*, which appeared in 1925. It was, I believe, the first film I ever saw, and the novel remains the most perfect example of its genre. In the movie, Professor Challenger was played by Wallace Beery (not otherwise noted for high-IQ roles) and the dinosaurs were courtesy of Willis O'Brien, the pioneer of stop-motion photography. This painstaking technique, of which Ray Harryhausen was the most famous exponent, has only now been made obsolete—like much else—by the wizards of Silicon Valley.

With all these memories crowding in upon me, I had no possible excuse to give Ms. Burns: I would simply have to accept her invitation.

There has, of course, been great progress in paleontology since Professor Simpson's death in 1984, and I am more than content to leave any updating to Stephen Jay Gould. I was, however, a little surprised to see that Sam Magruder's speculations about the future—from his viewpoint—extinction of the dinosaurs did not include what is now the best-known theory: asteroidal impact. Perhaps the manuscript was written prior to the famous paper by Luis and Walter Alvarez, "Extraterrestrial Cause for the Cretaceous-Tertiary Extinction," published in *Science* in 1980.

I was delighted to hear from Ms. Burns that her father was an admirer of my work, and wonder if he ever came across my own brief flirtation with time travel and dinosaurs. I had almost forgotten the short story, "Time's Arrow"—after all, it was written in 1946, a year which itself now seems almost prehistoric. And in reading through Simpson's novella, I began asking again, Is time travel really possible? Or must it always remain, as in my distant writings, fantasy? The classic argument against time travel is that it would allow a man to go back into the past and to kill one of his direct ancestors, thus making himself—and probably a considerable fraction of the human race—nonexistent.

Some ingenious writers, notably Robert Heinlein and Fritz Leiber, have accepted this challenge and said in effect: Very well—suppose such paradoxes *do* occur. What then? One of their answers is the concept of parallel time tracks. They assume that the past is not immutable—that one could, for instance, go back to 1865 and deflect the aim of John Wilkes Booth in Ford's Theater. But in so doing, one would abolish our world and create another, whose history would diverge so much from ours that it would eventually become wholly different.

Perhaps in a sense all possible universes have an existence, like the tracks in an infinite marshaling yard, but we merely move along one set of rails at a time. If we could travel backward, and change some key events in the past, all that we would really be doing would be going back to a switch point and setting off on another time track.

But it may not be as simple as this. Other writers have developed the theme that, even if we could change individual events in the past, the inertia of history is so enormous that it would make no difference. Thus you might save Lincoln from Booth's bullet—only to have another Confederate sympathizer waiting with a bomb in the foyer. And so on . . .

The most convincing argument against time travel is the remarkable scarcity of time travelers. However unpleasant our age may appear to the future, surely one would expect scholars and students to visit us, if such a thing is (will be?) possible at all. Though they might try to disguise themselves, accidents would be bound to happen—just as they would if we went back to imperial Rome with cameras and tape recorders concealed under our nylon togas. Time traveling could never be kept secret for very long; over and over again, and down through the ages, chronic argonauts (to use the original and singularly uninspiring title of *The Time Machine*) would inadvertently disclose themselves. As it is, the sole evidence of a security leak from the future appears to be the notebooks of Leonardo da Vinci. Their parade of inventions from succeeding centuries is astonishing but hardly conclusive proof that fifteenth-century Italy had visitors from elsewhen.

Some science-fiction writers have tried to get around this difficulty by suggesting that time is a spiral; though we may not be able to move along it, we can perhaps hop from coil to coil, visiting points so many millions of years apart that there is no danger of embarrassing collisions between cultures. Big-game hunters from the future may have wiped out the dinosaurs, but the age of *Homo sapiens* may lie in a blind region that they cannot reach.

You will gather from this that I do not take time travel very seriously; nor, I think, do most of those writers who have devoted so much effort and ingenuity to it. Yet the theme is one of the most fascinating—and sometimes the most moving—in the whole of literature, inspiring works as varied as James Branch Cabell's *Jurgen* and John Lloyd Balderston's *Berkeley Square*.

Even if we can never travel into the past, it has often been suggested that we could *see* into it. Strictly speaking, we never do anything else, because of the finite velocity of light. The image these words are forming on your retina left the page just about a nanosecond—one thousand millionth of a second—ago.

It is only when we look out into space that we see events that occurred centuries, or even millions of years, ago. This is a very limited kind of penetration into the past; in particular, it offers no possibility of seeing into our *own* past. We cannot hope that, when we have reached the worlds of nearby suns, we will find advanced races which have been watching us and recording our own lost history through super-telescopes. The light waves from any events on the Earth's surface are badly scrambled on their way out through the atmosphere—even when clouds allow them to escape at all. And after that, they are so swiftly weakened by distance that, even in theory, no telescope could be built that would allow one to observe terrestrial objects in any detail.

No creatures in a stellar system nine hundred light years away are now watching the Battle of Hastings. The rays that started in 1066 are, by now, too feeble even to show an image of the whole Earth. For there is a limit to the amplification of light, set by the nature of the light waves themselves, and no scientific advances can circumvent it.

If there is any way we can ever observe the past, it must depend upon technologies not only unborn but today unimagined. Yet the idea does not involve any logical contradictions or scientific absurdities and, in view of what has already happened in archaeological research, only a very foolish man would claim that it is impossible. For we have now recovered knowledge from the past which it once seemed obvious must have been lost forever—where the compass pointed ten thousand years ago; the temperature of long-vanished seas; the length of the Precambrian day.

Not long ago, such knowledge of the past would have seemed clairvoyance, not science. It has been achieved through the development of sensitive measuring instruments that can detect the incredibly faint traces left upon objects by their past history. No one can yet say how far such techniques may be extended; there may be some way in which all events leave their mark upon the universe, at a level not yet reached by our instruments (but possibly, under very abnormal circumstances, by our senses; is this the explanation of ghosts?). The time may come when we can read such marks, now as invisible to us as the signs of a trail are plain to an Indian scout or an Aborigine tracker. And then, the curtain will lift from the past.

The invaluable *Encyclopedia of Science Fiction* (1993) remarks perceptively: "Certain periods of the past have always attracted time-travellers because of their melodramatic potential. The Age of the Dinosaurs was inevitably the biggest draw—even to people who could only stand and stare, like the users of the time-viewer in [John] Taine's *Before the Dawn* (1934); it was later to become a favorite era for hunters, as in Ray Bradbury's 'A Sound of Thunder' (1952) and L. Sprague de Camp's 'A Gun for Dinosaur' (1956)." An ironic twist on this idea is a short story by Brian Aldiss, "Poor Little Warrior," when an intrepid sportsman, proudly examining his trophy, is promptly set upon and killed by its parasites. Have you ever wondered what sort of bugs would reside on a *T. rex*? They might be nastier—and certainly much more active—than those that infest whales.[1] I have never read *Before the Dawn* and am indebted to John Taine's biographer for the information that "through the invention of a 'televisor' a small group of men are able to view the Earth in the Mesozoic and to observe, ultimately, the last days of the dinosaurs," which Taine very implausibly endows with "human traits and values. . . . His hero, Belshazzar, is loyal, courageous and inventive. . . . In spite of its defects, *Before the Dawn* contains so many scenes of haunting grandeur that it has continued to grip readers."

Quite recently, some developments in cosmology have prompted a renewed interest in genuine time travel, and a number of scientists have even suggested that it might be theoretically possible to go into the past. However, the conditions needed to realize this are so extreme indeed, bizarre—that it seems unlikely that even a galactic super-civilization would allocate funds for the project. It would require such improbable feats as very precise navigation at the rim of a black hole, or stretching out a neutron star into a long cylinder whose surface was set spinning at the velocity of the light. And, even then, nothing larger than an atomic

---

[1] Although "A Sound of Thunder" is the classic treatment of the theme, David Gerrold's 1978 novel, *Deathbeast*, develops it in even more terrifying detail. And I highly recommend Allen Steele's 1990 story, "Trembling Earth," which is distilled *Jurassic Park*—and a clear case of telepathic plagiarism, since both appeared simultaneously.

nucleus could make the trip. So not even an amoeba would be able to go back in time to kill its—ah—grandfather.

C. S. Lewis once expressed the hope that space travel would be prohibited by God's quarantine regulations. He turned out to be wildly wrong; but that may well be true of time travel—at least into the past. There is no objection, of course, to movement in the other direction: we are all doing it at the rate of sixty seconds every minute, and could speed up the process by suspended animation. But anyone who goes Back to the Future will have to stay there.

Though I fear I have already intruded too much into what is, after all, an introduction to another author's work, I cannot resist adding one last personal note. Writing is a lonely profession, and after a few decades even the most devout egotist may occasionally yearn for company. But collaboration in any work of art is a risky business, and the more people involved, the smaller the chances of success. Can you imagine *Moby-Dick*, by Herman Melville and Nat Hawthorne? Or *War and Peace*, by Leo Tolstoy and Freddie Dostoyevsky, with additional dialogue by Van Turgenev?

Yet in being given the opportunity to write this introduction, I feel that I have indeed been involved in such a virtual collaboration, if not with H.G., then certainly with George Gaylord Simpson, and I am genuinely sorry that I never met either of them in real life. With these reflections, I am only too happy to oblige Ms. Burns with these prefatory words. And so here is *The Dechronization of Sam Magruder*, or, as I have privately titled her father's story, "A Crusoe of the Cretaceous," for that describes it exactly.

The
Dechronization
of
Sam Magruder

1

How
to Be
Alone

What would you do," asked the Universal Historian, "what could you do if you knew you were going to be utterly alone for the rest of your life?"

"That's something we'll never find out," said the Pragmatist. "The situation could not arise."

"Oh, I don't know," said the Ethnologist. "There were still some anchorites immured in Tibet not long ago."

"I've heard about that," said the Common Man. "They crawled into a little cave just big enough to turn around in, then pulled it in after them: walled up the entrance. Hasn't the human race finally gotten beyond that?"

"The human race never gets beyond anything," said the Universal Historian sententiously. "The popularity of peculiar practices changes from decade to decade or century to century, but there is always someone who keeps on doing or believing any conceivable action or creed, no matter how old or unpopular it may have become. There may still be a few immured anchorites in the Himalayas, but if so they are not really alone."

"How do you mean they aren't really alone?" asked the Ethnologist with some indignation. "Once they crawl in and the wall is built, they never see or speak to another human being."

"How are they fed?" demanded the Universal Historian.

The Ethnologist replied, "There's a small L-shaped tunnel through the wall, just a few inches wide. Every day or two someone outside reaches in the outer arm of the L and puts a bowl of gruel as far in as the length of his arm. Later the hermit sticks his arm in the inner branch of the L where he can just reach the bowl. But he can't see out and he doesn't even know when the outsider has come except that the bowl is there."

"Just the same, he's not really alone," the Universal Historian rejoined. "He has a contact with other men. Indirect, but still a contact. And his loneliness is not irrevocable. Any time, he could push a note into the L, saying 'Let me out of here.' He isn't so strongly tempted to ask to be let out just because he knows he can if he wants to. His being alone is always voluntary."

"That's what I mean," said the Pragmatist smugly. "There is no possible situation in which a man could be really and utterly alone without chance or hope of regaining contact with his fellows."

The Common Man said, "There have been castaways on desert islands who were never rescued, and there have been solitary rocket travelers who lost touch and were never heard from again. They were really and completely alone for the rest of their lives."

"You might say so," the Universal Historian agreed. "In a physical sense they were alone. It's also true in such cases that they remained, in fact, alone for the rest of their lives. But I was thinking of the psychological, the emotional situation. If you knew, knew with complete conviction, that nothing you did could possibly be observed by anyone else, would it seem worthwhile to do anything? If it were certain that no other human being would ever touch your existence, would you value that existence? That sort of thing. I'm sure that castaways live in hope of being picked up someday. Some lost rocket travelers have been rescued or have found a way back, and they said they had kept alive and kept trying to get in touch because they knew someone would look for them. They dared hope they'd see human faces again. They were not convinced of the reality and eternity of their loneliness. Certainly the same must have been true of the ones who were not rescued and who never did return. They did not abandon themselves to being alone, did not accept it as their fate. What interests me in this connection is the reaction of a man who lived with the conviction that he would surely never return to the human world or receive any word from it."

The Pragmatist said, "That's interesting to speculate about, I suppose, but it is idle speculation. We've none of us succeeded in thinking of a situation in which the possibility of getting back in touch would be beyond any desperate hope. Perhaps that could be for a man dying alone, and knowing he was dying, but that's a special and different case. It would be impossible for a man living alone, over any period of time. So I take it that the emotional situation of such interest to you is one that hasn't occurred and won't. I must say that a situation that cannot arise has no meaning for me."

"You're wrong about that," the Universal Historian said. "About the situation being quite impossible, I mean. I'll confess now that I've been leading you on since I introduced this subject. I had something up my sleeve. The situation of being hopelessly alone has arisen. There was one man who was absolutely and realistically sure that he would never have conscious contact of any sort with any other human being. He was right, and he did live out his last years wholly alone and with the knowledge of his fate. I know what happened to him, and I know something of how he reacted to it."

The Pragmatist laughed. "I was sure from the start that you had a good story for us. You usually do, in your own pedantic way, and sometimes the stories are true. I'm glad to have warning that this isn't one of the true ones."

"My dear sir!" The Universal Historian was all offended dignity. "You might at least have the grace to judge the truth of my story after hearing it, not before."

"Oh, come off it!" the Pragmatist shouted. "You remind me of the *true* story of the man who had heart failure and died in his sleep because he dreamed he was guillotined. Only the very innocent fail to ask how we know that's what he dreamed, since he died without telling. That sort of story is self-canceling. It can't be true, on the face of it. You preface your story with the statement that the hero could not and did not communicate it to anyone else, and that no one else was around when it occurred."

The Universal Historian affected a number of archaic customs and mannerisms. They were, I imagine, a by-product of his professional delving into ancient lore. At this point he silently and deliberately took out a tobacco pipe, such as I have seen in historical museums, and filled it with tobacco. (He obtained this, I learned on another occasion, from a botanical garden in the East Indies.) He set fire to the machine and began to puff smoke, which set the Common Man to coughing and was rather nauseating to all of us. Only after this obnoxious operation did he deign to answer the Pragmatist's sneers.

"My dear fellow," he said, "I have often had occasion to reprove you for your really slipshod use of language and your failure to attend to what is said. I did *not* say that the hero, as you call him, could not and did not communicate his experiences. I said that he was wholly alone and correctly expected to remain so, without conscious contact with other humans. He did, in fact, leave a communication on the wild chance that it might come to other human eyes. It did so, but not until any return communication with him was out of the question. I have seen his communication. Indeed I am currently engaged in preparing it for the press."

The Pragmatist was still full of fight and began raising new objections, but the rest of us quieted him. Our curiosity was aroused and we wanted the story.

"Who was he?"

"How did he come to be hopelessly alone?"

"Where was he?"

"What did he do?"

"His name," said the Universal Historian, "was Sam Magruder. What cut him off irrevocably from his fellow man was time, simply time. He found himself living some eighty million years before the human race evolved. His own life span was normal. Return to the Age of Man was impossible, as he well knew. The chances of his being joined by any other human were so infinitesimally small that the event could not rationally be expected, and Sam Magruder was eminently rational. Thus he was absolutely cut off from the rest of his race as no other man has ever been, to our knowledge."

"But what happened?"

"How did he get set back in time?"

"He was the victim of what is technically known as dechronization. In vulgar terms, he suffered a time-slip."

Hereupon the Universal Historian consulted his watch, another of his archaicisms, and announced that it was too late to continue the story that evening. Knowing that no power could make him go on until he chose, we had to accept his decision, and did so with bad grace. He made an appointment to meet us all several evenings later in his rooms at the Institute and promised to continue at that time.

2 Dechronization

At this point I am tempted to jump right into Magruder's own story, but I think that I had better give it to you in sequence, as we learned it. A certain amount of background is necessary in order to understand what happened, as nearly as it can be understood. The Universal Historian gave us much of this background at our second session, and I will give it here. This procedure has the advantage of permitting me to omit from the text of Magruder's narrative certain long explanatory notes inserted by the Universal Historian as editor. The Universal Historian can be stuffy enough in conversation, but as a speaker he remains halfway human. In a footnote his erudition is simply unbearable.

I resume, then, with our gathering in the rooms of the Universal Historian. It was evident that we were in for a lecture, and we were a little restive at the prospect, but our host made us comfortable in armchairs and proposed that we relax with drinks before talking seriously.

Another of his old-fashioned traits is that he likes to consume and to serve drinks containing ethyl alcohol. This substance, now a curiosity of the chemist's laboratory, was formerly consumed in large quantities. The initial effects are similar to those of synthetic inebrione, but continued consumption does not sustain euphoria. In large doses, ethyl alcohol produces depression and eventually coma. The coma generally passes after some hours, but it leaves distressing cerebral and gastric symptoms—what was known (the Universal Historian tells me) as a "hangover."

Forewarned by a previous experience with this insidious chemical, I had brought some inebrione tablets with which I insisted on preparing my own drinks. The others innocently accepted the Universal Historian's concoction, which he called, if I remember correctly, a "Mar-Teeny." I have reason to think that I am the only one of us who followed the Universal Historian's remarks clearly after the fourth or fifth round.

When we were all settled, our host began.

"The theory of dechronization, or of time-slip if you insist, is clear enough to the advanced students of the subject. In fact, this theory was largely worked out by Sam Magruder himself, for he was a research chronologist and one of the leaders in that field. In practice, time-slips must be extremely rare. Indeed there is no clearly established case other than that of Magruder. There is some irony in his being the unique victim of a natural principle that he discovered.

"I think it unlikely that you could follow the technicalities of the theory. Certainly the mathematics are beyond any of you. I confess that some aspects are a little beyond my own powers, in spite of the fact that my profession requires more than passing acquaintance with chronology. I may say that I have also had occasion to acquire considerable proficiency in paleontology. These qualifications have led to my being entrusted with the editorship of Magruder's communication. The connection with universal history and chronology must already be obvious, and that with paleontology will become evident when you read his story.

"The more technical and mathematical aspects of chronology are of no great importance for present purposes. Some of the simpler aspects are essential and perhaps are already more or less familiar to some of you from my own popular books such as *Timeliness and Timelessness, Ten Years per Second,* and the others. At least you already grasp the generally accepted view that there are two time universes. One has motion but is without time dimensions or growth. The other is motionless but has a single dimension and grows steadily in one direction within that dimension.

"The time-motion universe consists simply of the present. It is dimensionless because it has no extension of any sort. Obviously the present is a point in time and cannot include anything of the past, not even the last billionth part of a second. But this point is in constant motion. The present does not continue at the same place, so to speak, for any perceptible interval, no matter how short. All that is and really exists before us in the time-motion universe exists necessarily in the present, at a time-point. Hence it constantly and instantaneously flicks out of *this* reality, out of *this* time universe, into the other.

"That other time universe, the universe of time-dimension, might be said to consist of the past, but that is a crude way of putting the matter. The present cannot be measured. It has no duration. Our familiar seconds, minutes, hours, tendays, and years are measurements of the past. The past is linear. It has only one dimension and only two directions: away from and toward the present. It grows constantly, but in only one direction, toward the present. In fact, you might consider the present as the growing point of the past, much like the tip of a plant shoot that is steadily growing upward from the ground.

"The past has a reality, an objective and eternal existence, even more truly than does the present. It *produces* the present. The growth of the past is conditioned and determined by the whole of that past as existent up to any given present. Even intuitively, we feel that existence and reality demand duration. Yet the world of our senses, that in which we have our subjective beings, is the present, only, and is without duration. Duration demands eternal existence in the other universe, the time-dimension universe, or, to speak very loosely, in the past. It follows, of course, that the future does not exist and has no reality in any sense of the word."

Up to this point we had been enduring this lecture in Chronology 1 in respectful silence. Now the Common

Man, who had barely started his third Mar-Teeny and was only moderately fuddled as yet, could not restrain a remark.

"What about all these stories of time travel?" he asked. "I don't mean just the scientifiction stories, either, although I think they must have some basis. Only the other day there was a serious dispatch on the tele-news about a chronologist who was building a machine for travel into the future and who announced that it was about ready for trial."

"Pure twaddle!" exclaimed the Universal Historian inelegantly. "That's von Schrechlich, a known fool if not a knave. The best one can say is that he is deceiving himself. Anyone less charitable than I am might suppose he is bilking the Universal Research Foundation. And the scientifiction stories—which I never read, by the way—are mere fairy stories. The nonexistence of the future is a necessary conclusion from modern chronological theory, and you can't go traveling in the nonexistent. Not in real life, you can't."

The Common Man subsided.

"Now where was I?" continued the Universal Historian. "Oh, yes. There's just one other point about general chronology that should be mentioned. Once everything exists in the time-dimension universe, once it's materialized and incorporated by growth at the tip of the moving *now*, it naturally exists for good and all. All that ever happened is there, and everything is there all together, so to speak. It's hard to explain this non-technically. You can't exactly say everything exists *simultaneously* there—wrong use of a time term. But it all *is* there and continues to be there. Different events continue to exist but at different *places* in time, just as Chicago and Urania and Los Angeles all exist along the Central South Rocket Route, but at different places on it.

"Well, so much for general theory. That was all worked out by Saha'a, Uhr, and Day years ago and is common knowledge now. Let's get on to Magruder—"

" 'Sh about time," said the Ethnologist, who had turned somewhat pink and was waving his glass in the air. "Goo' ol' Magruder. Here 'sh 'a Magruder." He took another sip and closed his eyes.

The Universal Historian quite properly ignored this interruption.

"Magruder went on from there. He took it as fact that the two time universes exist and have the qualities I've suggested. He saw that everything and everyone normally have contacts with both. He asked, 'Now what would happen if a person, say, could concentrate himself in one or the other?' His answers were admittedly speculative, but they are reasonable. I have a file of his papers here, and I could read you the conclusions, but I guess you don't want to take the time—"

"Hic!" said the Pragmatist, or a sound to that effect.

The Universal Historian hurried on:

"Magruder decided that if you concentrated in the time-motion universe—or, you might say, in the present—you would just annihilate yourself as of that moment. The past produces the present, so if you stop contact with the past—no more production; no more you. But if you concentrated in the time-dimension universe? Then you'd disappear in the present, of course, and you'd be in a universe where everything, all of time up to now, all that ever happened, was right there with you. Yet that is constantly producing a *now*, a present, somewhere along the line. So Magruder speculated that you'd probably slip back into a *now*—but that the now might be at any time whatsoever! You might come back only a second ago. Then you'd probably never quite realize what had happened. Or you might come back a million or a billion years ago.

"Chronologists are now pretty well agreed that time started approximately ten billion years ago. Magruder figured that if you did have a time-slip, return to any time in that interval would be equally likely. Naturally that means that you'd be extremely unlikely to slip back anywhere near our times. You'd be almost sure to come back a long, long time ago, and then you'd be stuck with it." I think even he was feeling his ethyl alcohol or he would not have used so inelegant an expression.

"Whadya mean, stuck with it?" asked the Ethnologist. "Shlip back! Shlip forward!"

"But you see," said the Universal Historian, "you *can't* slip forward. The future doesn't exist in any universe. If you slipped to, say, a million years ago, then now, what is the present to us, would be nonexistent. You couldn't slip to it. If you slipped again, you'd slip still farther back. Magruder saw that. When he did slip, that's how he knew he was there for the rest of his life.

He could not possibly rejoin mankind, because where (or rather, when) he was, mankind did not exist in any time universe."

"Not alone, jush 'a same," belligerently remarked the Pragmatist, shaking his head a bit. "Magruder shlipped. So, far'sh he knowsh, shomeone *elsh* gonna shlip. Comp'ny, see? He'd think comp'ny might be comin'."

"That's a point," said the Universal Historian magnanimously, but went on to add: "Not a *good* point, however. There are ten billion years of time, as of now, to slip into, and one time as likely as another. Slipping is certainly extremely rare. If it weren't, we'd have heard of other cases—Magruder has a remark on that in his story, you'll see. Now, if there have been very few slips, and if they could turn up anywhere in ten billion years, what are the chances for two to turn up at the same time? —Not to mention at the same place! No. There was practically no chance at all, and Magruder knew that. He accepted it. He was alone, all right, and no hope at all for company."

"Oh, aw' righ'," agreeably said the Pragmatist. "Aw' righ'. No comp'ny comin'. I'm shleepy. Goin' home."

"I'm shleepy, too," agreed our host, then jerked himself upright and glared at us. "I am sleepy, that is. Good night, gen'l'men. Shame—uh—same time next week?"

Telenews

When we met again, a new member of the company was present. I knew it was not his first visit to the Universal Historian, because he had brought inebrione and politely refused ethyl alcohol drinks. So did all of us; my companions had learned the lesson. The new man was introduced as Pierre Précieux, and I gathered that he had something to do with the Magruder story. He had, as was to appear later.

"Look here," said the Pragmatist as soon as we had settled down. "I'm worked up about this Magruder, all right. I want to hear the whole thing. But that is what I want to hear. No more lectures. No more of your fancy introductions. If you've got the dope, let's have it."

He and the Universal Historian always did rub each other the wrong way. I expected a blowup, but the Universal Historian was in a mellow mood, for once, and he just smiled indulgently.

He said, "From now on someone else tells the story. Here's the first bit."

He laid before us a telenews printsheet. It was old, dated 30 February 2162, but was in good preservation. At the top was a big headline:

CHRONOLOGIST VANISHES

Under this was a picture and the caption:

Samuel TM12SC48 Magruder AChA3*

The picture, its colors still clear, showed a somewhat nondescript man, maybe forty or forty-five. Straight black hair. Well tanned. Small beard but no mustache. Large eyes. Yellow-brown irises. No epicanthus. Somewhat flattened nose. Perhaps the nose and the hair reflected the one-fifth mongoloid ancestry indicated by the middle-name symbols, but the caucasoid had predominated. Ancestors technicians and scientists. Top marks in citizenship school and in chronologists' professional school. Decorated three times for achievement. Quite a boy! They come better, but not much. Any of us would settle for an A-A3* to stick after our names.

The telenews story was clear enough, as far as the words went. Even with our preparation, the meaning back of the words was queer.

Samuel Magruder, 42½, distinguished chronologist, 1038 Upper Harlem, Zone 2A, S13 employee of the Chronological Institute, vanished yesterday at 1504:16 E.S.T. Up to that time, he was working in his laboratory, M14, Ramp J, at the Institute. His two assistants were also in the room: Hsuan Hsi, 28, S4, and Mary Lamb, 22, T6. Magruder was performing an experiment bearing on the quantum theory of time-motion, working at a bench near the middle of the laboratory. Hsi was reading a technical journal at his desk near the back door of the room. Lamb had just been sent by Magruder to turn on a ventilator near the front door. The two doors were the only means of exit from the windowless room, and both were locked to prevent interference with the experiment. One assistant was near each door and both swore that no one could have passed without being noticed. The keys were in Magruder's pocket and were later found in his clothes by the police, who broke down one door.

Hsi testified that his attention was attracted by an exclamation from Magruder, which he took to be "It *is* particulate!" This was at exactly 1504:11 E.S.T. (Both assistants were trained to note the precise time of any occurrence, as part of their chronological techniques.) Hsi turned and watched Magruder, who said nothing further. Lamb agrees as to the exclamation at 1504:11 E.S.T., but is uncertain as to its content, which she says may have been "It is too late!" She also turned to look at Magruder, and adds that his right hand moved downward, apparently on a switch activating part of the experimental apparatus.

Both witnesses agree that at 1504:16 E.S.T. Magruder seemed to slump rapidly to the floor. Both jumped to try to catch him. Hsi, arriving first, caught a sleeve of Magruder's laboratory smock, but the sleeve was empty. Lamb's testimony is that Hsi shook the sleeve for 1.2 seconds, then turned to her and exclaimed, "My God, Mary! The old man's done it!" Asked to clarify this statement, Hsi said that he had no memory of making it, that he was too shocked to take in what was occurring.

The two assistants rapidly ascertained that Magruder's clothing was in a pile on the floor but that Magruder himself had completely vanished. At 1506:43 Lamb used the interlabcom to ask the Institute communication center to call the police. A patrol, Adrian Sherlock, 36, Po4, in charge, arrived at 1512:01, found the doors locked, and broke in. Sherlock testifies that there was then no trace of Magruder in the room, which was thoroughly searched. Magruder's entire clothing was lying where he had been standing. All the zippers were closed, and the clothing was in the same arrangement as if being worn, pantisox tucked into the slippers, slippers latched, and so on.

The assistants were questioned and testified as stated above. A veritester showed that they were telling the truth as they saw it, and blood tests were negative for inebrione or sedihypnone. Asked for her suggestion as to what could have happened, Lamb stated that it was uncanny and that she intended to transfer to bioelectronics. Hsi stated that he thought Magruder had been dechronized, and referred to recent publications by Magruder. A colleague of Magruder's, Daniel Judgment, 53, S12, gave an opinion that dechronization is an erroneous theory and suggested that protoplasmic solvents be searched for in the laboratory. A search was made, with negative results.

The director of the Institute, Kto Znayet, 62, SA15, stated that Magruder's activities had hitherto been impeccable and that he was considered the top man in the special field of abstract chronology. Znayet suggested that Magruder had broken down as a result of overwork, but had no suggestion as to where Magruder had gone, or how. Znayet said that a memorial service would be held if Magruder did not reappear within a month, and that he personally would notify Magruder's widow and give her Magruder's separation allowance.

However, Magruder was unmarried but leaves a sister, Kathleen Yuan, 40, HW1, an adopted child, Fatima Magruder, 18, A2, and a dog, Caesar, 3½, Pe5. Magruder was AChA3* and was a member of numerous scientific, civic, and social associations, including the National Academy of Chronologists, the Society for Systematic Rectification, and the Harlem Hotshots.

Clipped to this account was another printsheet, dated one month later, with a small item marked at the bottom of one column.

SERVICES FOR CHRONOLOGIST

Memorial services were held today at the Chronological Institute for Samuel Magruder, 42½, S13, who vanished under mysterious circumstances on 29 February. The services followed a court decision that Magruder is legally nonliving and that permission be granted to administer his estate for the benefit of his adopted daughter, Fatima, and his dog, Caesar. Kto Znayet CChD1*, 62, SA15, director of the Institute, gave an address in which he eulogized Magruder's professional work. Znayet expressed the opinion that Magruder was the victim of foul play, and asked that a memorial be erected to this martyr of science. A half-hour holiday was observed at the Institute.

4 Discovery in the Desert

After we had all read the printsheets, the Pragmatist exclaimed:

"But the message, man, the message! We take it that Magruder disappeared. That proves nothing. There is even a hint in these news stories that something was held back, that instead of a time-slip Magruder may have been dissolved, purposely or by accident. These stories don't mean a thing unless you really have a communication from him after he vanished."

"We do have, as I told you," the Universal Historian said sternly. "Written after he vanished, from his point of view. Written long before, from ours."

"Double-talk!" said the Pragmatist rudely. "Let's see this communication."

The Common Man timidly agreed: "Yes, let's see it!"

With some annoyance, the Universal Historian said, "You shall see it, all in due course. This whole business is so extraordinary that it is going to be difficult to explain it to the world, or to make it credible. I am making a sort of trial run on you, and therefore I shall continue to present the matter to you carefully and in what I consider the proper sequence. The next point is perhaps the most crucial of all in establishing the authenticity of Magruder's story. That is the discovery of the communication. I've asked Pierre Précieux to come in and tell you about this. He made the discovery.

"To spare his modesty, I may say that Précieux is one of our leading geologists. He is BG1A2* and past president of the National Academy of Stratigraphy. His special field is the chronology, sedimentology, and stratigraphy of the Lancian Stage. In other words, he studies the age, nature, and succession of rocks laid down in western North America during the last part of the Age of Reptiles. But perhaps he will tell you about that."

"Thank you. I will tell as much of my work as is really necessary for us now," said Précieux in dry, somewhat clipped syllables. We were speaking Interlingual Swahili, of course, but I seemed to detect in his speech rather more than usual of some local accent. I judged that he might have originated in one of the relatively isolated Arctic communities. I later learned that this is correct: he came from a small mining settlement some twenty kilometers north of Permafrost Rocket Base.

"As you say," Précieux went on, "I have special interest in that part of Earth history when the great, grotesque reptiles were having their last, wild fling. My personal part is not the study of the reptiles, themselves. That must be left to my paleontological colleagues and in my case particularly to Saurier, who is Number Two in our Lancian Research Squadron. Besides giving general supervision to the squadron, my task is to study the rocks in which those last dinosaurs and their bizarre associates were buried. These rocks carry the time record of dinosaurian history, and they are the basis for reconstruction of the environment that spawned those monsters.

"Now, such rocks are found principally in the vicinity of the Rocky Mountains, and that vast region is the scene of our squadron's main field activities. Within the mountains themselves, the forces of erosion have destroyed most of the record. What remains is generally to be found in the high plains that start directly at the foot of the mountains or in the wider valleys and basins that lie between the various chains and ridges of the uplift. Twenty years ago, when the Lancian Squadron was first authorized, we started in the far north, on the shores of the Arctic Sea where the Rocky Mountain folds plunge into the frigid waters. Since then, we have been working systematically southward, and two years ago we reached the Province of New Mexico and Arizona.

"It had long been known that rocks appropriate to our quest occur toward the center of the desert area called the San Juan Basin. Expecting to spend several years in that region, we set up a comfortable permanent base camp at a place known as Ojo Alamo. 'Ojo Alamo' is an archaic name that has come down to us through some four centuries from the Spanish, one of several languages formerly spoken in that vicinity. The name means

'Cottonwood Spring.' Presumably it was appropriate when first applied, but now there is neither a cottonwood tree nor a spring there. There are traces of ancient human habitation, but the locality is now the center of a Registered Primitive Area and is open to no one except members of official squadrons licensed for research there.

"Our camp was—I may say 'is,' for it is still there—sheltered against a yellow sandstone cliff some twenty feet in height. We erected plastic domehuts for laboratories and living and sleeping quarters. Condensers supply water and chemibiotanks provide the luxury of nonsynthetic food, so that the whole small community is practically self-sustaining. Nuclear-powered helicopters have been used to explore the surrounding country over a radius of a hundred miles.

"The shale below the sandstone bed that rises above our camp also extends for long distances to the northwest and southeast. Ever since the twentieth century this striking geological formation has been known to represent in that region a final episode of the Age of Reptiles. In it occur the fossilized remains of terminal members of the races of dinosaurs. Above it are rocks in which dinosaur bones are absent and those of the earliest denizens of the Age of Mammals occur sparsely.

"Local drainage near our camp is to the southwest. In that direction is a broad zone of somber badlands. Almost completely devoid of vegetation and carved into myriad fantastic erosion forms, this landscape is as barren and as unearthly as the face of the moon, with which I can compare it at first hand. Pillars and pinnacles, deep, precipitous gorges, and labyrinthine, jagged crests have been carved by the winds and rains of millennia from a deposit of shales and sandstones known as the Kirtland and Fruitland formations, named after former settlements on the San Juan River, to the north. The scene is more grim than colorful. Many badlands are characterized by varied and vivid colors, but these badlands are painted in tones of gray or dull yellow. When this picture was composed, the pigments on Earth's palette were muddy and depressing.

"Yet to the initiated these dry and deserted badlands reveal a picture of riotous lost life. The deposits were laid down as much as eighty million years ago in ancient swamps and streams in which bulky dinosaurs splashed and over which flapped ungainly, toothed birds, while tiny furred and warm-blooded creatures watched timidly from hiding places in the reeds. The reconstruction of this scene and its integration into the long, long history of Earth and of life were the objects of our research.

"I have now explained our presence in that remote and uncanny spot, and I have pictured for you, in broad terms, the scene of my discovery. The discovery itself occurred on a hot afternoon six months ago. I was at that time toiling in the Kirtland badlands. My immediate task was to gather samples for analysis from a particularly persistent and uniform bed of dark gray shale. So free was this shale of foreign matter that I was surprised to find on its surface a broken slab of hard, almost quartzitic sandstone. I picked up this slab and found that it was covered with incised characters. At first this seemed to disperse the mystery. Early historic and archeological remains are not uncommon in that formerly inhabited region. An American explorer or an Indian resident had doubtless carved this memento of his passage there.

"Two things soon disabused me of this facile explanation. First was the nature of the message carved on the slab. Weathering had obscured the writing, and some fragments were missing, but I could make out enough to convince me that this was no commonplace scribbling but writing in a language I could read. The second and more startling discovery was that another slab was beginning to weather out of the undisturbed shale. No natural agency known to me could have introduced this extraneous object into so pure a bed of shale. With my prospecting pick, I quickly excavated the second slab and found that it, too, was covered with incised writing. Yet the insertion of this slab into the deposit must have been contemporaneous with the deposition of the mud now hardened into shale. In other words, the slab must have been placed there as much as eighty million years ago!

"I regretted having dug out this amazing relic without a witness to the fact that it had, indeed, been buried in shale undisturbed since the Cretaceous period. With my porticom I called all the squadron's other scientists to the spot. We excavated further, and in the course of the afternoon we turned up six more slabs. These were not only embedded in undisturbed strata, but also completely buried before our digging. These facts were witnessed by eight men of the highest reputation and with particular skill in distinguishing original from secondary deposition. We have their affidavits, which will form an appendix to the published version of Magruder's narrative.

"Extensive search failed to reveal other slabs, and indeed a quick check of the text suggested that we had the whole series. One of the slabs clearly began the message. The others seemed to form a continuous sequence and, as it happened, the first slab found was the end of the story. The writing on the buried slabs has been made fully legible by judicious cleaning. The final, weathered slab is partly obscure but the text can be recovered with few uncertainties.

"The find was evidently outside the special field of our own researches. After consultation within the squadron, with the Geological Institute, and with the Scientific Coordinating Authority, it was decided that the Universal Historian is best qualified to study the slabs and to prepare a definitive, annotated text for publication. In this work, already virtually completed, he is of course receiving such cooperation as is needed from me and from other specialists, notably Saurier, as regards the life of the period, and Schreiben, on paleographic matters."

Précieux's fluent and well-organized account of his part in the amazing story had held our attention firmly. Now, as he ceased speaking, there was a little stir in our group. Feet were moved. Throats were cleared. Our host took up his pipe and puffed an obnoxious cloud of tobacco smoke. The Ethnologist tossed off the remainder of his glass of inebrione citrate. The Pragmatist leaned back and, as might be expected, was the first to recover speech.

"The slabs!" he exclaimed. "Let's see the slabs!"

The Universal Historian, agreeable at last to the complete revelation, unlocked a durone cabinet that stood against one wall of the room. The interior was fitted out with eight sliding shelves, on each of which was a thin plate of pinkish, fine-grained sandstone.

"You can handle them," the Universal Historian reassured us. "They have all been treated and are now unbreakable and unscratchable."

We handed them around, marveling at the minute, clear characters engraved on them. The Pragmatist clung to the slabs as they were passed to him and began reading them hurriedly, but the Universal Historian firmly removed them from his grasp.

"I have prepared a text," said the Universal Historian, "and have a copy made for each of you. You are quite free to satisfy yourselves that my text is a correct transcription from the slabs, but you will find it more convenient to read the narrative from your copies. So far, I have copied out the first six slabs for you. I will give you copies of the other two at a later date."

The text is as follows. As I promised, I have omitted most of the Universal Historian's scholarly but dull annotations. I have also omitted Précieux's formal account of the discovery, Saurier's essay "The Life of the Late Cretaceous, with Special Reference to the Observations of Samuel Magruder," and the six appendices. I have occasionally excised some of Magruder's remarks when these seemed repetitious, offensive, or unnecessary to the story. Otherwise the account that I shall give here is substantially the same as that of the full, official text to be published by the Universal Historical Society. Except for matter placed in brackets—[ ]—and Chapter 11, the following pages are in Magruder's own words.

5

Magruder's Narrative.

Slab 1:

The Time-Slip

My name is Samuel TM12SC48 Magruder AChA3*. Good old Sam Magruder. Odd that I should want to put down my names and titles first, or to put them down at all. Names are to distinguish us from other men, and I am the only man who exists or ever has existed. Titles are supposedly to label our capacities, really to try to impress our associates. The qualifications of AChA3* have not much bearing on my present life, and my associates here are definitely not impressed. But there it is: I cling to being Sam Magruder. I want to reassure myself that I *am* I, that this is the same being who is to be born 80 million years from now and registered as Samuel TM12SC48 Magruder. Yet *that* person does not really exist in any time dimension or universe. He is only *going to* exist.

Undoubtedly my disappearance was—or, I should say, will be—noticed. There will be an inquiry, and Hsi may know enough to put them on the right track. Not that it will do me or anyone the slightest good to know that I disappeared by dechronization. It does, at least, prove my theory. I try to get from that such bitter satisfaction as I can.

After the first shock, the moment of undiluted astonishment, I realized at once what had happened. I was spared that puzzle by the fact that dechronization is my baby. Perhaps no one else would have recognized it—but perhaps it happened to me just because I was mucking about with the subject. I need not explain it here, even though I kid myself that this may be read, that I may be writing to somebody. If this record is found much before 2162 A.D., they (you, the reader) will not know enough about time to understand any explanation I can give. If it is discovered around 2162 or later, you will find almost all I can tell you in my published papers. Perhaps if you are much later, you will know more than I do on the subject, but I have some reason to doubt that.

[At this point the Universal Historian has inserted a footnote, seven pages long in fine type. He gives a complete bibliography of Magruder's scientific publications and a professedly "semi-popular" explanation of time-universe and dechronization theory.]

The one thing you will not know is what I was doing when I slipped. I suppose that may be important so I had better mention if briefly. I was trying to determine whether the present, the moving point of the time-motion universe, moves continuously or in little jumps.

It seems to move continuously, but we all know how worthless our unaided perceptions are in such a case. The quantum theory has taught us that light and other forms of energy are not continuous. My idea was that time, also, might be discontinuous, a succession of time quanta, with timeless discontinuities between them. Of course the jumps would be so small (so *brief*, you might say, if they were not timeless) as to be below the threshold of time perception.

My technique was to magnify time, to slow down perception of it to such a point that extremely short intervals would become evident. I used a Langsam decelerator with certain modifications of my own, greatly increasing its power. When the slip happened, I had just started a run in which I was going to slow down a millionth of a second so that it would be perceived as five hours—in effect a magnification of 18 billion times. I started the deceleration gradually and had gotten up to perhaps ×100 million when I began to notice a strange and rapid flickering sensation. This elated me. I was sure I was actually beginning to perceive the discontinuous, particulate flow of time. I got excited and shoved down the control to full power, and—wham! The laboratory was gone and I was up to my waist in mucky water.

I think part of what happened was that the deceleration was so great as nearly to stop time, and that this hit where I was *between* time quanta, where there was no present for me to be in. That shoved me wholly into the other time universe, the time-dimension universe. I bounced right out, but not at the same place. Not by some eighty million years!

It cannot really be that simple. There is some other complication that I do not know and that no one will ever discover. If it were just a matter of high deceleration at the right moment, then after I developed the modified Langsam decelerator, which was or will be in 2162, anyone could time-slip at will. This is a desperate experience, but there are always plenty of people eager to do anything thrilling and unusual. They would certainly have filled up the whole of time with time-slippers. We would by 2162 have had all sorts of evidence of them and messages from them throughout geological history. The fact that there was no such evidence whatever in 2162 means that time-slipping is never going to be common or to be produced at will. I may very well be the only case in all history.

I have batted this idea around a great deal since I slipped. Naturally I wanted to kid myself that there is some chance of meeting another human here. No soap! It is a dead cinch that I am the only human in the universe now, now in the late Cretaceous.

[Here the Universal Historian has inserted another long note that seems to me not merely humorless, as usual, but also officious. He apologizes for what he calls the "flippant colloquialism" of some of Magruder's language, "so unbecoming to one of his scientific stature." Then he quotes many of Magruder's acquaintances to the effect that Magruder "meant nothing by it" but was likely to slip into lower vernaculars especially when excited or deeply moved. To illustrate the point, he adds passages from twenty-three of Magruder's personal letters.]

As I said, I landed up to my waist in mucky water. I was naked as a newborn baby. The time-slip did not work on my clothes or anything around me. It would not have mattered much, anyway, since all I had in my pockets were keys and some money, not exactly useful in the Cretaceous. The clothes themselves would have been useful at first, but would not have lasted long.

I let out an involuntary yell of surprise. There was a tremendous splashing and thrashing about on the other side of some reeds. I started wading over, partly to investigate and partly because I could not think of anything else to do and felt silly just standing there. The bottom was sticky black ooze. In places I sank in so I was afraid I would be bogged down, so I swam till I came to the reeds. I groped with my bare feet and found a little relatively solid footing. I parted the screen of vegetation; the saw-toothed edges lacerated my hands.

From the waters in front of me arose what might have been a bright green, oversized fire hose. Perhaps two feet in diameter where it emerged from the water, it tapered to about half that in the fifteen feet of its exposed length. It ended, not in a nozzle as I almost expected, but in a head of sorts. The head was wedge-shaped in profile, and a crimson eye glared near the top.

Behind and below the eye was a smaller, black earhole. The mouth, open in what looked like a vapid grin, was rimmed with white, pencil-like teeth.

I did not immediately identify this apparition. I should have, because my training in chronology included a stiff course in paleontology, but I was laboring under two inevitable disabilities. In the first place, I had not yet located myself even roughly in time. A swamp could occur at any time since rain began. I knew, by now, that I had slipped into what had been the past for me, into time before 29 February 2162, but how far back? It could have been no more than a few months or it could have been into the dim and lifeless mysteries of the Archaeozoic Era. I had to expect anything whatever, and I had no frame of reference for any more explicit expectation.

The second difficulty in recognition arose from the limitations of paleontological restoration. The colors of prehistoric animals are unknown. Playing it safe, artists have not dared to use the emerald-green hue of the creature I now saw before me. They show the eyes as brown or black, not the startling crimson of the reality before me. My mental image from student days was all the wrong colors. Would you immediately recognize a bright red, stripeless tiger or a purple-spotted squirrel?

The critter and I stared at each other for what seemed like a long time. It never did identify me, but I finally got it placed. It was a dinosaur. Among the numerous kinds of dinosaurs, large and small, it was one of the sauropods. No others, even in that race of giants, reached quite the size implied by the emergent neck of this monstrosity. No others had such long, hoselike necks, such small heads in relation to their overall hugeness, or such discrepant pencil stubs for teeth.

I was not at all frightened. I am no braver than I have to be, but the sight was so interesting that I did not think of danger. Then I remembered that the sauropods were, are (in my peculiar circumstances I am never quite sure what tense to use)—that they are vegetarians. Doubtless my new acquaintance would lash back if I annoyed it, but at least it did not view me as a potential snack. I gave an experimental shout, and sure enough it startled and went splashing off, waving its neck in alarm.

The encounter was stabilizing for me. You have no idea how disorienting it is not to know, even approximately, *when* you are living. I had already worked up considerable anxiety as to the time into which I had slipped, and this creature gave me a fairly good estimate. At least I thought that it did, although I have since decided that I was a few scores of millions of years off the mark. Here was one of the large sauropod dinosaurs, possibly a *Diplodocus*. Their heyday was in the late Jurassic, perhaps 140 million years before 2162. So that, more or less, is where, or rather when, I decided I was. Later I saw so many species that I knew to be much later in age that I had to revise my estimate. This is certainly the late Cretaceous, not the late Jurassic, and only about 80, rather than 150, million years before the time from which I slipped. Evidently the sauropods survived much longer than I remember from my professional school days, or perhaps the paleontologists of 2162 have slipped up on this point.

[Here there is a note by Saurier which strikes me as rather more enlightening than most of those by the Universal Historian. Saurier explains that Magruder's sauropod was undoubtedly a Cretaceous *Alamosaurus* and not a Jurassic *Diplodocus*. Pioneer paleontologists did, indeed, think that the sauropods became extinct soon after the late Jurassic. As early as the twentieth century, however, it was discovered that they continued into the late Cretaceous in more southern and probably warmer areas. *Alamosaurus* was first found near and was named for Ojo Alamo, where Précieux's camp was situated and in the region where Magruder passed the Cretaceous part of his life. Magruder's course in paleontology may have skipped this detail, or he may simply have forgotten it.]

When the sauropod had ponderously gone its way, I began to think a little more rationally about my situation. It was desperate enough, but I did not then think it quite hopeless. Crowding to the back of my mind the worst forebodings, I saw getting to dry land as the first necessity. In most directions the great lagoon stretched to the horizon, but far off to my left I could see the tops of palm trees. I had an idea that these usually grow on land, and anyway there was no better choice. I started walking and swimming in that direction.

It was a long, hard struggle for a body still used to the laboratory rather than to physical activity. The distance must have been four or five miles. Now that I know the lagoon better and have seen some of its more blood-thirsty residents, I cannot understand how I ever emerged alive. A little luck must have been doled out to me in return for the desperate bad luck of the time-slip. I met no other living thing from the time the sauropod left to the time I stumbled, exhausted but whole, onto the low land under the palm trees.

6

Magruder's Narrative.

Slab 2:

The First Day

Why, from the start, did I think it worthwhile to survive? Why am I still struggling for survival after years here alone? I never thought in that other time, my time among men, that merely surviving had any value. The value of life was in many things. First of all, learning, investigating, probing the secrets of nature and making her workings known for the benefit of mankind. That was the deep purpose of my life. Then there was a host of great, but lesser, satisfactions. Reading, especially. Music. Companionship and talk. Good food. Travel.

What have I now and what will I ever have, for as long as I live? Reading, music, companionship?— Pardon my hysteria! Scientific study? I have thought that over more carefully, tried to find some outlet or incentive there. But living as I must, there is little time for contemplation. I have no instruments, no laboratory, no library, none of the requirements for profound research. I am limited to simple observation. True, everything I observe has never been and will never be seen by another human being. But I cannot pass this on. It benefits no one else. Oh, I can put some of my observations on these slabs and I can pretend I am communicating them, but I know I am fooling myself. There is a chance in a million that someone will read this someday. I will never know, however, and here I have learned that benefiting mankind is at the same time a social and a selfish occupation. It is no good unless you see the benefit and get some sort of approval for it. And, in fact, as I think it over, I have not seen much that the paleontologists and geologists will not know in the twenty-second century. My observations could not help them greatly. No, science certainly does not sustain me here.

Travel? Am I kidding! I have taken such a journey as no one ever dreamed of, and it turns out that I never did like travel for its own sake. What I liked was going places *with* someone, meeting new kinds of people, coming back and talking about it all. No, I never liked travel, and I certainly do not like this little trip.

Food? Phooey! You know the old crack about living to eat or eating to live. Here it is eat to live, and no nonsense about it. You have to be starving to be able to swallow some of the messes I must eat if I am to live. So I guess it is lucky that I am starving half the time. Blood and guts! Leaves to swell my belly and make it stop rumbling, but they go right on and make me hungrier than ever—

[Magruder continues in this vein for several more paragraphs. His most violent emotions seem to have become concentrated on this subject of food. The passage is highly repetitious, and part of it is too strong for *my* stomach. If you want it all, plus a haughtily disapproving footnote by the Universal Historian, read the official edition. I skip to where Magruder goes back to his story.]

That first day was a honey! At least I do not have to go through that again.

I got to the palm trees, and I lay down under them flat on my back, pooped to the world. I thought I would die right there, and at first I did not care. In utter exhaustion, I began to sniffle with self-pity. I had not cried since I was a year old, and long habit made me hold it in for a while. Then I yelled out loud, "Go on and cry, Sam! Good old Sam! Who the hell cares? So you're too proud to cry! Pride is your face for other people. Look around! Look at all the other people! Don't let them see you cry, Sam!" I must have bawled for an hour, at least. I felt a little better for it.

Then I felt hungry, and the old urge to survive began to stir.

I thought, "Well, Sam, here you go. You've always thought that man arose by the survival of the fittest. You've got more brains than anything else in the universe and your species is the top answer to the question of survival. Allez-oop, Sam! Let's see you survive."

There is a pretty big catch to that, as I have learned. It is *mankind* that has survived, not any one man. The fitness includes and depends on social organization, on cooperation, on division of labor, on the building up and passing on of knowledge, of tools and methods. Among most of the successful higher animals, survival generally depends on a group, a family, or a herd. The sole individual hasn't a prayer without his group. I am cut off from my group completely. I am not in the world my species is fitted for, and I am surrounded by hungry animals whose world this is, who are fitted for it. I arrived here with nothing but my bare body and my brains, brains adapted to a society that will not arise for 80 million years and used only to working through implements to be invented in that society.

I argued with myself. The habit has grown on me. I talk to myself almost constantly now. Why not? It is a comfort, and there is no one else to talk to.

"Buck up, Sam!" I said. "Man's the most *adaptable* animal, too. He never had to adapt to anything like this before, but let's have a shot at it. Don't bellyache just because the situation is not that in which AChA3* brains work best. You've still got them and they must be *some* use to you."

There was no fruit on the palm trees. A little farther back from the water was another grove of trees. I am not a botanist, and the species must certainly have been different from anything growing in 2162, but they looked like magnolias. They had buds, but the buds did not taste good and I still was not hungry enough to eat anything that tasted bad, just to get a feeling of something in my stomach. There were no shrubs or herbs or anything under the trees, just bare ground.

Vegetable food did not look promising, so I started thinking of animal food. I would have to kill something, although the sauropod was still the only animal I had seen and I knew I could not manage to kill one of those. (I never have, although I think I could now if I put my mind to it.) If I was going to kill any animal, I would need a weapon. I decided to make a bow and arrow. That was a foolish thing to start with, but I still had a lot to learn and I was still confused and upset by the whole affair.

For a bow, I needed string. I tried braiding and twisting reeds from the edge of the lagoon, but they had no strength at all. I shinnied up one of the palm trees. I skinned my arms and legs and belly till I was a mass of blood, but I managed to tear loose some of the dead fronds that hung below the crown. I jumped back down to the ground and turned my ankle. I tore fibers loose from the palm fronds and broke my fingernails down to the quick, and beyond. I made a string, of sorts. I broke a branch off one of the magnolias, if that is what they are, bent it a little, and tied the string from one end to the other. I broke off a smaller branch, more or less straight, and chewed one end until it was a little sharp. This broke the cap off one of my incisor teeth—I had an appointment to go to the dentist, on 30 February 2162, the day after I slipped. I put the blunt end of the little stick against the string, pulled it back gingerly, and let go. It flew about ten feet and stuck in the dirt. I had a bow and arrow! I felt pretty proud.

A little lizardlike thing came wandering along. Food! Excitedly I gave a big pull on my arrow against the bow string and let fly. The string broke. The bow broke. The arrow hit hard dirt about two feet from the lizard, and the arrow broke. The lizard flicked into a hole between some roots. I lay down and cried my heart out.

While I was still crying, the sun went down. The air, which had been balmy, became cool. I lay there, bleeding, aching, and shivering for what must have been hours, until I finally sobbed myself to sleep.

7

Magruder's Narrative.

Slab 3:

First

Successes

In my peculiar situation, you would imagine I would spend most of my time thinking about people I knew before the time-slip, the friends, relatives, and loved ones I am never to see again. I did at first. People walked through my confused dreams that first night, and I woke up thinking about them. I left no wife. I loved a girl once and we had some happy times together, but we never got around to marriage. We drifted away from each other, finally, and parted friends. Thinking back—or forward—from the Cretaceous, I tried without much success to be pleased about this. She would have been terribly grieved if we had been married and then I had vanished like that. I had an adopted daughter. I was very fond of her and I think she liked me all right, but she will not miss me much, and frankly I do not miss her as much as I do most of my friends. She was away at citizenship schools most of the time, of course, and I was someone to pay the bills and to indulge her when she came home on vacations. When the time-slip came, she was old enough to be interested mostly in boys and had no time for me. That is normal, and it was normal, too, for my interests to move away from her as she developed away from me. I miss my colleagues. I miss my friends. I miss them terribly and the ache persists as the years pass, but I no longer think much about them. The daily hazards of life demand most of my attention, and I have carefully schooled myself to give as little time as possible to regrets that are vain.

I did not yet feel like that on my first morning. My daughter, my sister, my dog, the director, my assistants, my cronies were so vividly present to me that I saw them with the force of painful hallucinations. I ached in every muscle. I was covered with dried blood and half-formed scabs. During the night some fiendish swamp insects had bitten my unprotected hide from head to foot. Every bit of me hurt, and I could hardly move.

In a way the second morning was even worse than the first afternoon, but I remember less about it. I think I suffered less just because my situation was so desperate. I became light-headed and hysterical. I believe I was quite out of my mind for hours. I do remember going again through the whole painful, laborious process of making a bow and arrow. It broke, as had the first one. I think I remember laughing madly and repeating the process over and over: making one bow and arrow after another and purposely breaking them as soon as they were made.

It was a bright day, and my noon I had a crowning

misery. I was severely sunburned. I blistered all over, and I must have developed a high fever. When I returned to my senses, the insect bites and the sunburn persuaded me that for a pale, thin-skinned, furless mammal, clothing might be as necessary for survival as food.

I did return to my senses. I was shocked back into them sometime during the course of the afternoon by my first sight of a tyrannosaur and by another close shave I had at the shore of the lagoon. Looking back, the haze of my memory clears with me standing in the magnolia grove, watching something move between me and the lake. It was a reptile, a dinosaur fifteen feet high as it poised on its ponderous hind legs, thirty feet long from its obscene snout to the end of its great, tapered tail. This was no inoffensive hulk of a herbivorous sauropod. It was a carnivore, and it saw meat. Its small, two-toed hands were held up beneath its tremendous jaw in a way that might have seemed ludicrously ladylike if the intention had not been so obviously grim. Its teeth were six-inch daggers and gleamed white as it swung its ponderous head to face me. In a sort of hypnotic horror, I thought inconsequentially, "But your teeth should be dark brown!" I had often seen the tyrannosaur skull in the Universal Natural History Museum, and its teeth were deeply colored. I had never stopped to think that the discoloration was the result of mineralization and that in the living animal the teeth would be white, as they are.

My impulse was the same as yours would have been; I wanted to turn and run. Fortunately for me, the

Tyrannosaurus rex

pumping adrenaline in my bloodstream threw my tortured muscles into spasm. I was literally rooted to the spot. I could not have run during that moment if my life had depended on it, as, indeed, I was sure it did. The awful monster launched its charge, and still I stood impotently. Only as it loomed directly over me, its whistling bellow resounding in my ears like the trumpet of doom, did I recover volition enough to leap to one side. Unable to throw so much momentum into a swerve, the tyrannosaur thundered by, knocking down the small trees as if they were herbs, and finally skidding to a stop twenty yards beyond me.

My weakness had led me unwillingly into the one tactic by which a man may safely face a tyrannosaur. To run would be to die, for who could outrun that tremendous animal machine? But by the grace of physical law, man's two hundred pounds can dodge agilely while the tyrannosaur's five tons must continue straight on or only slowly change its course. Before a charging tyrannosaur, you have only to step aside and let the mountain of flesh go by. I cannot conquer a thrill of horror whenever one of these obscenities comes in view, but since that first charge they have been less dangerous to me than flies. I need not even worry about them while I sleep. Like that of all dinosaurs, their sluggish reptilian metabolism requires external warmth to stoke their fires. They are quiescent in the cool night air and do not stir dangerously until the morning sun has limbered them.

You see why I cannot serve you as a man of science? I am the only human being who knows how to cope with the mighty *Tyrannosaurus rex*—but I am the only human being who will ever have to!

After that first charge, I correctly expected a return, but I had already grasped the secret of defense. In command of myself now, I stood until the futile mountain of demoniac flesh was upon me, then dodged and watched it crash onward toward the lagoon. When it finally stopped, I was hidden among the few trees still standing. It looked about aimlessly. Obviously its tiny reptilian brain had lost all memory of what the excitement was about. It wandered about for a few minutes, then loped off around the shore and out of sight. I rejoiced in being *Homo sapiens* and marked up one score for our side.

Many a lion hunter has been killed by a tsetse fly. It is too easy to think that the biggest enemy is the most dangerous. I was to learn that the carnivores my own size and smaller were the ones I must really dread. My first lesson came almost immediately after my triumph over the tyrannosaur and served to dampen over-confidence.

When the tyrannosaur had gone and my heart had stopped pounding, I went down to the shore of the lagoon to drink and to wash my wounds. Most of the shore was a long, muddy slope where you could hardly tell the point at which wet mud became muddy water, but I found one clump of scrub willow that bordered deeper water and that gave fairly good footing. I clung to a handful of willow and dipped the other hand, open-fingered, to test the temperature.

There was a swirl, a snap, a tremendous tug, and an excruciating pain, so immediate and so simultaneous that I did not separate the impact on my various senses but perceived the sequence as a single, instantaneous event. The willows held, and my scream and leap backward also blended into the shocking surprise. When time seemed to start flowing again, I was standing back of the willows several feet from the shore, looking with unbelieving eyes at my right hand. Where the little finger had been, there was only a bleeding stump.

Fortunately one of my broken childish bowstrings was not far away, and this served well enough as a tourniquet. Palm-fiber string has never been of any other use to me (now I use dinosaur tendons for bowstrings and cord), but it saved me from bleeding to death. The lesson turned out to be cheap after all. The stump pained me acutely for days, but it did not become infected and finally healed well. The awkwardness passed, and in a month or so I was hardly conscious of missing a finger.

Creeping back gingerly to the shore, I could make out my disappointed assailant in the murky water. It was a crocodile, only about five or six feet long, but quite big enough to have dragged me under had it not miscalculated enough to grab a finger instead of the whole hand. It looked, as far as I could see, exactly like crocodiles in zoos in 2162 A.D. There is a successful adaptation for you! Already some tens of millions of years before my world of 80,000,000 B.C. crocodiles had evolved, and henceforth to our, or I should say your, own day they changed hardly at all.

It has been said by some theorists that cases like that of the crocodile, virtually unchanged for 100 million years and more, represent a failure of the evolutionary force, a blind alley, or a long senescence. As I gazed at my antagonist, it occurred to me how false this is. Here was no failure but an adaptation so successful, so perfect that once developed it has never needed to change. Is it, perhaps, not the success but the failure of adaptation that has forced evolving life onward to what we, at least, consider higher levels? The crocodile in his sluggish waters had perfectly mastered life in an unchanging environment. No challenge arose. Our ancestors lived in a more evanescent world, where what was adaptation at one time became an inadaptive burden in 100,000, 1,000,000, or 10 million years. For them, their adaptation was always a blind struggle to keep up, to face new conditions, to exploit new opportunities. Only changing races met that challenge. Of the others, those to whom chance closed the adaptive avenue of change, the unlucky became extinct and the lucky, like the crocodile, found and settled into some way of life where the challenge was absent, and there they stagnated.

—Part of this philosophizing is, of course, the product of later, more leisurely thinking, but something of all this did flit through my mind at that moment of desperation and misery. Shock and long habit seemed to turn attention briefly from the unbearable immediate scene to its eternal significance. My needs and my urges soon, however, overbore philosophy.

Again I went to the water's edge, but this time down a sloping shore where the water was too shallow to harbor a crocodile or other serious enemy unseen. The water was muddy and somewhat fetid, but it was sweet and it quenched my thirst. Here, too, I found my first food. A plant like a water lily, uprooted perhaps by a carelessly browsing sauropod, had stranded nearby. It bore succulent bulbs. These are harsh to the teeth and insipid to the taste, but they are filling.

It seemed that fate (in which I do not believe except as a symbol for what we do not understand) had decided that my abject misery had gone on long enough, or that it should be prolonged by being tempered with endurable intervals. Other and better food came to hand while I was still wolfing down water lily bulbs. A small turtle crawled out of the water nearby. Its capture was no problem. I killed it by jabbing the point of one of my broken arrows into the body through the opening alongside the head. Bleeding was profuse and would have nauseated me in my other life. Now it stimulated my appetite. I broke the shell by beating it against a tree trunk. The tenacious, cold-blooded creature died hard. The pierced heart was still twitching when I pulled it out and gulped it down. It was delicious.

[Here the Universal Historian has an apologetic note. I was tempted to omit this passage from the present version, but I must not wholly obscure the rawness of the world in which Magruder lived. It seems important, too, to remember that civilized man remains capable of brutality.]

Temporary satiation of my hunger and thirst stimulated my inventiveness in other directions. It occurred to me that the reeds, useless for cordage, were ideal for matting. I gathered a great bundle of them. Straining my memory back to childhood days, after some fumbling I managed to weave two mats. One, about eight feet long by three wide, I pierced with a slit near the center. When my head was poked through the slit, the mat hung down in front and in back, protecting most of my body while leaving my arms free at the sides and my legs unencumbered below. The other, smaller mat became a hat, tied on by loose ends sufficiently strong for this purpose.

I had defended myself against two of the most rapacious carnivores of the Cretaceous—or at least, I had evaded them with no more loss than that of one finger. I had found and eaten food, of a sort. I had clothed myself, after a fashion. Survival became conceivable. I still itched and ached all over and my wounded hand hurt like hell, but I felt pretty good.

8

Magruder's Narrative.

Slab 4:

Tools and Fire

I am not going to tell the story of each day of my long stay here. I kept no diary, and during the first year I did not even count days. Now I have a satisfactory calendar of my own and always know the date by my own system. This comes from my long training as a chronologist, no doubt, but it is useful, too. I have my dates for moving up into the hills before the spring and autumn floods cover the lowlands, my date when the figs are ripe in *Pentaceratops* Valley, my date for turtle-egging, my date for catching the annual migration of coelurosaurs through the pass, and so on. I know my way about now, and I have life pretty well systematized. Apart from the annual rhythm, most days are pretty much alike, and I have no wish to record all my petty and routine adventures.

The first two days were the most crucial ones, so I have set them down in some detail. That second night, I was really over the hump already. I was going to survive for a while, at least. Not but what I still had plenty of crises coming to me. I am still hungry often enough—a great deal too often. I still have narrow escapes at unexpected and frequent moments. But I haven't completely panicked after that second day. I have not seriously doubted that I could learn to cope with whatever came up, barring a quickly fatal accident—which cannot be barred, of course, but you see what I mean. Since then I have had a sufficient feeling of confidence, and mere blind fear of my environment has not plagued me unduly.

The first few years were one long learning process in the toughest school on Earth. I made plenty of blunders, but I learned fast and I learned well.

For several days I hung around the shore near my first landing point. It was soon clear that the resources there were very limited and this was no place to settle down. Before starting out, however, I wanted to get myself toughened up a bit and to try to lay up some sort of provisions for an exploring trip. The supply of turtles and lily bulbs held up well enough, and I got so that I could occasionally spear a fish with a sharp stick. I found that fish and turtle meat would remain edible for several days if torn into shreds and dried in the sun.

What I wanted most of all was fire. I wanted to cook meat. I wanted to warm myself at night. I wanted to bake clay pots so I could carry water. I wanted the friendly glow and the feeling of protection that comes from fire. What a futile education I had had! Even matches were old-fashioned to me and I had resorted to them only when all else failed. As for really practical methods, all I could think of was the old crack about rubbing two Boy Scouts together. I did try it with sticks and rubbed and rubbed for the greater part of a day. The sticks got warm, all right, but nothing else happened.

Since I could not make fire and could not then think what else to try, I gave it up for the time being and moved stones to the top of my priority list. Next to fire, tools and weapons were the biggest need. Sticks broken off with my hands were tools and weapons for a start, but of the most primitive and inadequate sort. To have any hope of raising my standard of living—or of continuing to live at all for very long—I needed something better, and that meant stones, for a start. Here by the lagoon the soil was all fine silt and clay, without even small pebbles. So the purpose of my first exploration was simply to find a good, hard rock.

I know now that you could wander for weeks, even months, in most directions here and never see a stone. The whole region is low, recently emergent from the sea, and most of it is an area of swamps and muck, or sand, at best. I had luck in that my first attempt to find stones was successful, but the kind of luck that rewards a rational approach to a problem. I had to follow a stream, because I had no way to carry water. Many streams entered the lagoon. I scouted them for several miles each way along the shore. One was cooler than the others and had a sandier bottom. I also found that it several times had freshets when the other streams were unaffected. I reasoned that such a stream was likely to flow from higher land than the others and that higher land might mean rocks.

The trip took six days. I covered only about seventy-five miles because I had to travel slowly. I stopped for hours to try to spear fish or to find other food in order to conserve my inadequate supply of dried meat. My feet hurt badly and had to be rested occasionally. Reed mats proved to be entirely inadequate as sandals. I did not yet have leather or sinews or any way to work wood. I was also interrupted frequently on my trek. I was charged by tyrannosaurs three times. One was most persistent and kept me dodging him for an hour before he gave up. I saw two others at greater distances and lay down quietly until they wandered away. Then I met for the first time one of the really dangerous carnivorous dinosaurs, the species that still is my greatest trial. I take it to be one of the smaller gorgosaurs. Not much bigger than a man, it can twist and turn almost as well. Dodging it is far more difficult and hazardous than side-stepping a tyrannosaur. In build, it is rather like a tyrannosaur: bipedal, long-tailed, with tiny front legs of no real use except to grasp and steady prey while the great teeth slash. It is more slender and agile than a tyrannosaur, even for its size, and the head, although still large, is relatively less immense.

Fortunately I was near a tree when this creature started after me. I had not climbed a tree for thirty years of my interrupted lifetime, but I got up that one, and just in time. The beast could not climb, but it charged the tree several times and then squatted under it, squint-

Gorgosaurus

ing an expressionless, merciless, vivid yellow eye at me, waiting for me to drop into its horribly effective tearing machine. I did not move, and it finally forgot I was there and went off in search of other prey. That is one universal trait of dinosaur psychology: they seem to have practically no memories at all. They never persist at anything, because they forget what it was. I have seen one surrounded by food, eating industriously, suddenly forget what it was up to, wander around vaguely for a while, stumble by accident on the food it had left, and resume eating voraciously as if a long and worthy search had been rewarded. If you can stave them off long enough and break off action, they will usually forget you and leave you alone, provided you do not move too soon and start a whole new episode. That is one of the things I was already learning on my first long trek.

—I suddenly remember that I have not mentioned the hadrosaurs. I take them so much for granted that I assumed that any reader of this would know that they were there in swarms, paddling along the stream or chomping on reeds alongside it. They are grotesque and bulky enough, but quite inoffensive. They are bipedal, as are the carnivorous dinosaurs, and the largest of them reach the size of a tyrannosaur. Their build and habits are, however, quite different. Their long, tapering tails are flattened from side to side, not round in cross section as in tyrannosaurs and gorgosaurs. Their great hind feet do not have claws, but hoof-like or nail-like terminations. Webs are present between the toes. The front legs, also with webbed feet or hands, are much larger than in the carnivorous dinosaurs. The hadrosaurs are more at home in the water than on land. They scull along using all four feet as paddles. When in a real hurry, they get up speed with powerful, undulatory strokes of the flattened tail.

The hadrosaurs' heads have a flattened, scooplike beak which has led—will lead—to their being called duck-billed dinosaurs, but the so-called beak is covered with scaly skin, not with a horny bill, so that the living creatures do not in fact look at all like ducks. They are strict vegetarians. Vast quantities of water plants, reeds, and the like are gathered in by the large scoop, chopped to bits by a battery of sharp, shearing teeth in the sides and back of the jaws, and then swallowed. As they feed, there is a constant chomping noise, and a group of hadrosaurs eating reeds can be heard afar.

There are at least a half dozen different sorts of hadrosaurs in this region. In the well-watered lowlands they are much the commonest reptiles—or, at least, the most

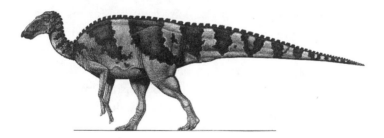

Edmontosaurus annectens, a hadrosaur

obvious. Some of the small lizards and turtles may be more abundant, but their incomparably smaller bulk makes them less noticeable. The different species of hadrosaurs vary somewhat in size and in color, but the most apparent distinction is in the head. Some have the top of the head flat. Others have an elevated, comb-like, fore-and-aft crest. Still others have a remarkable prong-like projection curving upward and backward.

[Here Saurier has a note in the official text. He points out that the function of these crests is unknown to modern paleontologists and has been the subject of long controversy. He is greatly annoyed that the only man ever to see a living hadrosaur failed to describe the crests adequately and said nothing whatever about their function. He suggests, however, that the function may be implied in Magruder's too brief remarks. Magruder speaks of the crests as the handiest means of distinguishing among the various species. Saurier speculates that this was perhaps their real function, that they were signals by which the hadrosaurs recognized their own kind.]

Near the lagoon, the stream I was following mean-dered sluggishly on the flat, marshy bottomland. On the second day of my journey upstream I was already in a definite, although broad and shallow, valley. The water-course was straighter and the flow visibly more rapid. Thereafter the valley became steadily deeper and more definite. On the fourth and fifth days I was traveling through low hills covered with rather scrubby vegetation. The stream bottom is pebbly here. None of the pebbles is large enough to be of real use, but I was encouraged to think that I was approaching a source of hard rock. On the morning of the sixth day I came to a gorge where the stream had carved a deep, narrow passage through a somber vertical wall of stone.

[Précieux notes that this was probably a basalt dike. He believes that Magruder's course was generally north-ward and that he was approaching the San Juan uplift, in what is now the mountainous region of southwestern Colorado. The uprearing of the present 14,000-foot mountain rampart was later in date than the time of Ma-gruder's residence there, but there is evidence that gen-tler elevation had then already occurred.]

I made my way through this gorge with some diffi-culty. It is so narrow in places that the only passage is wholly occupied by the stream. There I had to wade painfully in the chill and rapid water, in danger of stum-bling and being dashed against the rocks by the swift current. I later learned that the gorge is impassable most of the time, because at any but the lowest stages of flow

the water is too deep and fast for wading. I have therefore had to develop another and still more laborious
route, climbing over the ridge a couple of miles east of
Black Gate, as I have named the gorge.

When I had finally won my way through this barrier,
the country opened out before me into a broad and
beautiful valley in the hills. My later annual routine
made me a migrant in search of seasonal food over a
large area perhaps a hundred miles or more across.
Within this territory I now have established places of
residence at a dozen strategic spots, from the low shore
near where I first landed up to the elevated pass at the
head of *Pentaceratops* Valley. This valley is, however, my
favorite spot. This is home. My forced trips to other
stopping points are excursions away from home and into
alien landscapes.

I do not believe that I can portray the valley in words
as I see it in reality. It stretches some ten miles from
Black Gate, at the lower end, to Coelurosaur Pass, at the
upper end and perhaps a thousand feet higher in elevation. Down the middle flows the swift, cool stream,
crystal clear except when in flood. The water is too
rapid, too chill, and too shallow for hadrosaurs or crocodiles, and none of these occur above Black Gate. The
absence of crocodiles makes the stream safe for bathing,
a luxury that adds greatly to my delight in the valley.
There are numerous perchlike fish and a few small turtles, both welcome sources of food. There were also
freshwater clams, so succulent that I have improvidently
almost exterminated them.

The valley is rimmed by high hills all around. Black Ridge closes its lower end completely except for the perilous passage at Black Gate. The Coelurosaur Mountains loom purple at the upper end. At the sides are rolling hills covered with forests of trees resembling redwoods and oaks. The broad valley bottom between these hills and the stream is mostly open country but has scattered, noble groves of palms and figs, other sources of tasty and nourishing food in season.

Near the lower end of the valley, a mile or so above Black Gate, a series of low, rocky ridges runs down from the west to within a hundred yards of the stream. Here I found what I was looking for, and more. Along the ridge is an outcrop of hard, brittle rock that I judge to be quartzite. In the streambed at and above this point are pebbles and boulders, up to a foot or more in diameter, of an extremely hard, tough, fine-grained, varicolored rock that may be jasper.

[In a note, Précieux vouches for the probable accuracy of these identifications.]

Here I had found an abundance of the raw material for which I was searching! Here, too, was unexpected bounty: near the end of the ridge I found a rock overhang beneath which was a dry, shallow recess, an ideal shelter from wind and rain. I took possession of this at once. It is my home. Over the years I have greatly improved it. Now it has a mud-and-stone shelter wall, a fireplace, and a store of bowls, tools, weapons, robes, and dried food. Even on my first night in the valley, when this was nothing but a bare hollow, it became home to me.

The next morning I awoke at the first glimmer of dawn. Near the foot of the ridge I almost stumbled on a coelurosaur, lying in a huddle, benumbed by the cool of night. The animal did not stir while I ran to the stream, picked up a jasper boulder, and crept back again. I crashed the boulder down on the creature's head, and it died with convulsive thrashings of its sinewy legs. This triumph, my first important kill, not only gave me several days' supply of meat but also added to sticks and stones three other essential raw materials: hide, tendons, and bones.

With appetite sated by raw meat, I gathered together a pile of quartzite and jasper at my shelter and began pounding and chipping, trying to fashion the rock into useful implements. At first such little success as I had was purely accidental. Since then I have steadily improved by practice, and within a month I could make a workable arrowhead, spear point, or knife in ten or fifteen minutes, seldom spoiling one. My first efforts were incredibly crude, however, and even now I cannot rival the fine Paleolithic points to be seen in the archaeological museum of the twenty-second century.

It would bore me and any possible, improbable reader of this record to tell in detail of my slow progress in toolmaking and of the way in which I finally managed over months and years to provide a full armament. I shall only mention some of the more important items that I did eventually create. Axes, my favorites both as tools and as weapons: stone heads hafted to wooden handles with coelurosaur tendons. Bow and arrows, the arrows stone- or bone-tipped and feathered. (But I must add that bow and arrows remain for me more of a pastime than an essential weapon; I make few kills with them and rely far more on axe and spear.) Spears of several specialized designs: heavy and stone-tipped, for serious combat; long and slender, with hooked bone prongs, for spearing fish; well-balanced throwing spears, without separate points but with the end sharpened and fire-hardened, for small game. Stone knives. Scrapers for working wood, as for spear shafts, and for cleaning skins. Bone awls for working leather and furs, piercing them for sewing with tendons. Wooden spoons for stirring and drinking broth. Baked clay pots for cooking and for water carrying and storage. Wooden mallets and fine stone points for inscribing the record I am now writing.

My clothing, too, has become far more practical and sophisticated than my first spring outfit of reed matting. I continue to use reed or palm-leaf hats, but now I have several soft, warm robes of fur and of feathered bird skins, besides a lighter jacket and breeches of supple leather, tanned with a mash of fresh brains. I have moccasins of tough dinosaur hide and, for rocky terrain, sandals with wooden soles tied on my feet with leather thongs.

From what I have said, it is evident that I did finally obtain fire. I got it first within a month of moving into the valley. Lightning struck and kindled a tree near my shelter. I tore off a burning branch, carried it quickly home, and kept the fire alive for several weeks by constant attention. Then one day I ranged too far, was away from home overnight, and to my consternation found the fire dead on my return—that was one of my really bad moments. Pounding rocks sometimes made sparks fly and I tried for days to start a fire in this way, but I never succeeded. Finally I went back to wood-rubbing and tried a dozen expedients to make this effective. The device I finally worked out may be pure invention, or may be based on subconscious memory of some museum exhibit.

[The Universal Historian notes that the device was well known to primitive man and that Magruder was probably right in his second surmise.]

My fire maker has four pieces: a slab of rather soft wood, a blunt-pointed shaft of hard wood, a round stone with a small depression on one side, and a short bow with a rather loose leather bowstring. The bowstring is twisted twice around the shaft. The shaft is placed upright with the lower end in a notch in the slab, which rests on the ground. The stone is then held at the top end of the shaft, pressing this down firmly with the left hand while the right hand rapidly pulls the bow back and forth. This rotates the shaft rapidly. Friction heats the slab and finally produces a glow in tinder piled at a strategic point. With this device, I can now make fire within four or five minutes whenever I want.

—While writing this last passage, I have been thinking how extremely clever I am. "Quite a boy, this Sam!"

I keep saying, as I think how well I have provided everything a person could possibly want. But then I start thinking of the "absolute necessities" of life in the twenty-second century, and I realize that I have none of them, not a single one. I have only the most absurdly primitive substitutes for a very few of those that really *are* necessities. And I have not been really comfortable, in any sense of comfort as future man will know it, for a single moment since I slipped into the Cretaceous.

9

Magruder's Narrative.

Slab 5:

Dinosaurs

When I was a kid, I was crazy about dinosaurs. I guess most boys go through that stage. I used to haunt the dinosaur halls of the Universal Natural History Museum and spend awestruck hours gazing at the colossal framework of *Brontosaurus*, the terrible teeth of *Tyrannosaurus*, or the grotesque awkwardness of *Triceratops*. I also devoured comic books in which dinosaurs figured and had a small library of scientifiction specializing in stories dealing with the three great periods of dinosaurian dominance: the Triassic, Jurassic, and Cretaceous.

This half-forgotten boyhood hobby, along with an almost equally half-forgotten professional-school course in paleontology, gave a certain sense of familiarity to the Cretaceous when I found myself living in that period. Many things seemed subtly similar and yet, in clear detail, sharply different from something I had seen before. It was like seeing in reality something of which I had previously dreamed. I think that this greatly aided my early adjustment to life amid scenes so bizarre and so savagely alien.

Most comic-book and scientifiction stories involving dinosaurs rely on constant conflict for such interest as they have. Their version of life among the dinosaurs is one of quick and gory battle every time there is a meeting between two of the monsters—and, of course, their dinosaurs all are monsters. Every dinosaur encountered instantly attacks any human character in such stories. I find the reality quite different. There are battles, gore, and attacks, but these are merely episodes. Real-life dinosaurs pass most of their time eating, sleeping, and mating, as do most animals. The great majority of them are herbivorous and never attack unless they believe that they are menaced. Some dinosaurs are truly monstrous, of course, but as I have already indicated, these are actually among the least dangerous to man. Many dinosaurs are really quite small. The coelurosaurs are, on an average, lighter than I am and there is one species that probably does not run over forty or fifty pounds at most for the oldest and toughest bulls.

So much for the difference between sensational fiction and real life among the dinosaurs. It remains true that some dinosaurs are dangerous and that all are endlessly fascinating to me.

Two kinds, abundant in my home valley and of major importance to me, have been mentioned but not described: *Pentaceratops* and the coelurosaurs. I call my vale *Pentaceratops* Valley because of the abundance of these creatures in it. They are bulky, four-footed animals,

Pentaceratops sternbergii

ranging up to twenty feet or so in length from their beaks to the tips of their rather stocky tails. The body and legs are elephantine. The heads are relatively enormous, five or six feet in length, with a saddle-shaped bony frill, covered with heavy skin, extending back over the short, stocky neck. The front of the head terminates in a sharp, toothless beak, hooked somewhat like that of a hawk or eagle. Chopping teeth for cutting food, exclusively vegetable, occur further back in the jaw. Two sharp horns arise one above each eye and another, more stocky horn is present at the midline on the nose. So far, *Pentaceratops* is very like its relative *Triceratops*, more familiar in books and restorations. It differs in having two more horns—or sharp spikes, at least—projecting outward on the sides of the back part of the head.

Pentaceratops is a vegetarian, but it is a somewhat bothersome neighbor just the same. It is surprisingly agile for so large an animal and has the habit of charging at sounds, head down and horns thrusting at what it takes for an enemy. This defense by offense is doubtless a reflex useful in dealing with the tyrannosaurs and large gorgosaurs that occasionally prey on these brutes. To me, the habit is something of a nuisance. It has become a commonplace for me to be proceeding about my own business in the valley when there is a sudden thudding of heavy feet and a series of gasping roars. Another *Pentaceratops* has heard the rattle of a stone at my passage and has blindly charged. They are almost as easy to evade as tyrannosaurs, but it is annoying to have to be prepared to dodge at any moment.

The herds of *Pentaceratops* live in the valley the year around. The agile coelurosaurs, on the other hand, are seasonal visitors. They spend the winter here, and they summer in the highlands back of Coelurosaur Pass, which I have named for them. Each spring they migrate up through the pass. Each autumn they return. It is a grand sight to see the whole floor of the pass covered with their teeming thousands, all hurrying along in the same direction. The migrations provide two of the fixtures in my annual schedule. I go to see the spectacle and also because it is an opportunity to kill a dozen or so of the animals. Among the dinosaurs, they are my favorite prey. The meat is unusually appetizing. The hides are light and supple, a quality unusual in dinosaurs, most of which have skin like armor plate. The tendons are strong and easily worked, providing my best cordage.

Coelurosaurus

The coelurosaurs are bipeds. They run swiftly on their long, slender hind legs, with their skinny tails held up and waving behind them. The short front legs, used for grasping, are clawed and rather gorgosaurlike. The heads are small, but with large and brilliant eyes. The mouth, usually foolishly agape, has small teeth or none. Their only defense is flight. They are moronic even for dinosaurs, and it is relatively easy for a determined hunter to stalk them. As long as he is not visible, they think themselves safe and with luck can be overcome by a quick dash from cover and a slash with a hunting spear. With their skinny bodies and low metabolism, they are also even more affected by chill air than other dinosaurs and are sluggish and somnolent on a cool morning—this was the downfall of my first victim among them. They are ready prey for the gorgosaurs, as they are for me, and are the mainstay of the gorgosaur diet. Thousands are consumed each year, but they are prolific and other thousands soon take the places of the slain.

Speaking of their being prolific, I may say that coelurosaur eggs, which they lay each spring in the sands of the uplands just beyond Coelurosaur Pass, are delicious when fresh. Most other dinosaur eggs have a somewhat musty, unpleasant taste and are a last resort as food. Turtle eggs, when obtainable, are much better. Scrambled turtle eggs are perhaps my favorite food, although one I usually have for only a few days each year.

Such are the lords of creation here in the Cretaceous. There are other varieties of dinosaurs here, of course, but I have now mentioned the more numerous and striking sorts. There are also a great many animals other than dinosaurs, and I shall later make particular note of a few of these, but this is truly an Age of Dinosaurs. They dominate most of the scenes among which I live.

A major topic of paleontological discussion in the twenty-second century is, or will be, the extinction of the dinosaurs. "Here, Sam," I used to tell myself, "is a wonderful opportunity for a real contribution to science. You know that all these swarms of dinosaurs are nearing extinction. The Cretaceous is drawing to a close, and when it ends, so will all these reptiles. You know the fate that is in store for them. Here you are, living among them. If you can't find the reasons for their extinction, you must be pretty dumb."

Well, it turns out that I am pretty dumb. I have studied the dinosaurs for years and brooded about their approaching end, but I cannot see any presage of it and cannot imagine a reason. Some students say (or will say, in that far future twenty-second century) that dinosaurs became extinct because the weather grew too cold. It is true that nights are usually cool here and that the dinosaurs all feel this. Without exception, they are sluggish and relatively inactive at night, but they soon pep up after the sun rises. There has been no frost during all my years here, even in the highlands. I would guess that the lowest temperature I have experienced has been around 45 degrees. That feels chilly, all right, especially after a sunny day with temperatures probably in the 80s or low 90s, but it is far from lethal, even to a dinosaur. As a matter of fact, the big dinosaurs are less affected by the chill of night than the small ones. I suppose they are simply so bulky that it takes them longer to cool off.

That brings up a point that I could clear up for the paleontologists if I could communicate with them. In the latter part of the twentieth century one of them had— will have, I mean—the idea that dinosaurs might have been warm-blooded like birds and mammals rather than cold-blooded like their closest twentieth-century relatives, the crocodiles and alligators, and all other reptiles of that time. In fact the usual terms "warm-blooded" and "cold-blooded" are misleading because the real point is that some animals, those called warm-blooded, have internal temperature control and their bodies stay at about the same temperature within a wide range of temperatures around them. Others lack such control and, except for the effects of exercising, their body temperatures go up and down with the external temperatures.

Those are the so-called "cold-blooded" ones, although on a hot day their blood may be hotter than that of a "warm-blooded" animal. Now that I am living among dinosaurs, I know that they are all cold-blooded in the usual sense of that word—or are poikilothermal, to put it more accurately and more technically. The idea that they might be—have—been warm-blooded (homoiothermal) had—will have—a lot of publicity for a while just because it was touted as sensational news. There really was no evidence for it, and when it ceased to be news it was quietly dropped.

Some of the paleontologists who believed, correctly as I now know, that dinosaurs were cold-blooded or poikilothermal had another theory, or guess, about their extinction that was just the opposite of the view that their extinction was caused by cold. They said—will say (I still have trouble with tenses in my peculiar relationship to time)—that the dinosaurs became extinct because the latest Cretaceous climates were too warm for them. The theory is that heat built up in their bodies and, in particular, that it made them sterile so that they finally failed to reproduce. Again, there is no evidence here for such a thing. The climate is not unduly hot, subtropical at most. My dinosaur neighbors are certainly not sterile. They breed with great abandon, and virtually all of their numerous eggs are fertile.

Still another theory is that the little, furry, warm-blooded mammals (about which, more later) caused the extinction of the dinosaurs by eating their eggs. Here, at least, I can make a definite negative contribution.

Mammals do *not* eat dinosaur eggs. Period. Coelurosaurs do sometimes eat the eggs of other dinosaurs, or even their own eggs, but this has no apparent effect on the population. And it is as hard for me to see how dinosaurs could cause their own extinction by eating each other, or each other's eggs, as to see how people could make a living by taking in each other's laundry.

Disease is a possibility, of course, but if so it will be some terrific epidemic still in the future for me. The dinosaurs here are remarkably healthy. They finally die violent deaths, or waste away in great old age, and seldom succumb to disease. There was one epidemic that struck the coelurosaurs just after their autumn migration. Perhaps a quarter or a third of the flock was stricken. They were dying all over, suddenly twitching in spasms and dropping into a rigor from which they never recovered. But next autumn, when they came down from the highlands again, they were as numerous as ever. More of the young had survived than in usual years.

Meanwhile, here the dinosaurs are, vigorous, prolific, seeming to be in their heyday and without a hint that extinction is just around the corner. In short, I know no more about the causes for their disappearance than if I had never seen one.

What can I say that will help the paleontologist of the future, if any should chance to see this record? Little or nothing, really, beyond confirmation of the cold-bloodedness of the dinosaurs. Perhaps my most solid help in other respects can be to artists who may restore these animals. At least, I do know their colors.

[Here follows a detailed list of all the dinosaurs known to Magruder, with the colors of each species. The list seems to me to have no general interest. Those professionally concerned can consult it in the Universal Historian's full, official text.]

10 Magruder's Narrative.

Slab 6:

Brooding

My real purpose in engraving these slabs is a search for comprehension. Primarily, the search is for my own sake. I want to understand what has happened to me and why I have reacted as I have. I am exploring my own nature, and perhaps also the nature of mankind, of the great species of which I stand here as an advance sample. Secondarily, I cannot entirely abandon hope that these words will sometime be read by other humans. I know how slight is this possibility. I also realize that I am never to know whether this message reaches others of my kind. Yet I take some small and irrational comfort from the bare chance that my desperate voice will be heard, that someone, sometime, will be aware of Sam Magruder and will feel interest in, perhaps sympathy for, his fate.

I have just reread my last two slabs, and it seems to me that they are rather beside the point for my purpose. They are necessary for comprehension, but they do not in themselves tend toward that goal. What I have done and what I have seen are essential parts of the story, of course, but the only really important thing is what I have felt and thought. This is much harder to convey, but it is the essence of my story.

I have said something of the desperation of the crucial first days. Thereafter came the period when I was physically so busy working out a way of life that I had little time for thought of anything but the immediate situation. I was then relatively free either of fear or of despair. This condition lasted for some months and then slowly gave way to a complex emotional state that has settled on me permanently. Its steady background is melancholy, a dully aching sadness, for which there is no remedy but death. The melancholy is tinged with wonder, with attempts to find some meaning in my life. Intermittently there are episodes when I give way to acute despair and horror. Less frequently as the years pass I briefly recapture the relative emotional ease of my first months, becoming engrossed in a present situation without thought for past and future. This happens sometimes in the excitement of the chase or of combat. On occasion, I have deliberately sought forgetfulness by picking unnecessary fights with the more ferocious of my neighbors. I once sought out and finally killed a tyrannosaur. It was an epic struggle. I do not narrate it here simply because it means nothing as regards comprehension of my existence. It was, in fact, pure escapism from the emotional realities of this life.

Most other forms of escape, or even of simple diversion, are of course denied here. The favorite relaxation of the twenty-second century, teleshowings, is merely an annoying memory to me now. For reading, art, and music, I have only what I myself create. These slabs are at present the only reading matter on Earth, probably all there is in the universe. Sometimes I try to remember in detail, to recreate in my mind, the great classics of literature, but I am not very successful. In these bizarre surroundings, forcing attention to the future classics requires painful effort. Painting and sculpture are of no use to me. I have no talent for them and defective memory of the masterpieces I have seen. Music is better. I have good auditory imagery, and sometimes as I lie awaiting sleep I can hear the majestic strains of a symphony. I have made myself some instruments: reed whistles or flutes, panpipes, and even a primitive sort of stringed instrument, a sounding board beneath tense dinosaur gut, plucked with a gorgosaur claw.

I have one other important diversion, the simplest of all: looking at scenery. I have always been a sensitive admirer of nature, and goodness knows I have enough of it around me here. The sunsets can be gorgeous, especially when one of the volcanoes to the north of Coelurosaur Pass has erupted recently and there is ash in the air. The ego struggles hard, and there is even some satisfaction in the thought that no other human being has seen or will ever see these landscapes in their varying moods.

The satisfaction is a melancholy one. Melancholy! It lies too near the surface for any of my few diversions to subdue it wholly or for long.

My change of mood, the beginning of this long sadness, dates from the Great Delirium as much as from any one episode. In general, I have been remarkably free of disease. No colds, no flu, none of the transient and minor but enfeebling illnesses that still beset us in the twenty-second century in spite of the wonderful success of medicine in virtually banishing the more serious and chronic ailments. I believe that most of the viruses and microbes that are to attack mankind have not evolved yet, here in the Cretaceous. They await the host, *Homo sapiens,* to which they will be specific. Yet protoplasm is much alike in dinosaurs or in men, and some agents of disease are less particular. I did have one very serious illness, which I remember with horror as the Great Delirium.

This happened during my first winter in the Cretaceous. I was settled in *Pentaceratops* Valley. One morning I awoke in my shelter with a splitting headache and with a vague memory of unpleasant dreams. I threw some wood on the fire, roasted a fresh coelurosaur drumstick, and tried to force down some nourishment. The little I could swallow was immediately vomited. My muscles ached and I was soon on fire with fever. I dragged myself to the stream. (I had no pottery or water containers as yet.) There I collapsed and blacked out.

In my next confused memory, I was back in my shelter and it was night. Embers of my fire were still glowing and I thought vaguely that I should add fuel, but the effort hardly seemed worthwhile. All at once, I heard a shout. Not the hoarse rasp of a benumbed *Pentaceratops* or the mournful cry of a toothed bird, but a human call. My heart leapt and I tried to answer, but could not.

I came to again, as it seemed, with strong arms around my shoulders and a voice saying, "Here, old man, drink this!" Some fiery liquid trickled down my throat from a flask.

"I declare, Sam," said the voice, increasingly familiar, "you are in bad shape. But don't worry. Everything's all right now. I'm going to fix you right up!"

"Oh!" I said joyfully. "I know you now. You're my father! You're Dad, aren't you?"

"Of course, Sam," he said.

"Thank God!" I said. "Oh, thank God! I've been lonely. So lonely."

I slept.

Whenever I roused a little, I could hear the dear, familiar voice.

"Sam, do you remember the cabin we had in the mountains, where we used to go fishing together?"

"Sam, your mother's been a little worried about you. You should find time to write her oftener, Sam."

"Sam, do you remember when we lived in Des Moines and there was that little girl with yellow curls next door?"

"Sam, where have you put your hood and gown? It's almost time to go to the commencement exercises."

"Sam, Lilian is here and wants to see you."

"Sam, ———" "Sam, ———" "Sam, ———"

And I would drop off again, to dreams more confused or finally to welcome blackness and annihilation as in death.

How long this went on I do not know. Finally came a morning when I awoke fully.

"Dad!" I cried, "I feel so much better! I think I'm getting well! Dad—" And I suddenly realized that my father was not there, and had not been. In the Cretaceous, he would not be born for eighty million years. In the twenty-second century, he was to die ten years before my time-slip. He was lost to me, as completely, irrevocably lost as all other human beings.

I would never see him or my mother, or my sister, or Lilian, or Fatima, or anyone else, except in delirium.

I was alone. Starkly, hopelessly, eternally alone. Alone I remain, and must to the end.

Then I wanted to die, but I could not. The fever had passed. I was alive and I had to take up the burden of life again.

"Why?" I asked myself. "Why must I? It will be easy and painless to lie here until I starve. I don't even feel hungry now, just weak. Why bother ever to eat again?"

"Now, Sam," I replied to myself. "You know you can't do that. You're the only human being in the whole universe and you have to survive just as long as you can."

I crawled back to the stream and drank. I dragged myself to the shelter and ate from my scanty and half-putrid store. I hated myself for making the effort, for not letting myself die, but I nursed myself back to strength again. I have had to go on living.

Everything must be done. Food must be found and eaten. Implements must be invented and made. Fire must be kindled. Attackers must be evaded or fought. None of this is worth the trouble, because no one is here to see. There is no one to tell of the day's work and adventures when I return to my shelter at night. It is merely silly to attend to myself when there is no one else to care whether I do or not. But it has to be done.

Loneliness has so many aspects. You cannot, surely, imagine it if you have not experienced it. Take sex, for example. I am the only member of my bisexual species in the universe. I am a male for whom no female will exist for many millions of years—long, long after I am gone. Much of the time I am so tired, weak, and hungry that I have no sex drive to bother me. Occasionally I am in physical well-being, and then sex may become an obsession, the more acute because its normal gratification is an absolute impossibility.

[At this point I am impelled to omit a rather lengthy passage. Magruder's discussion becomes so frank that its inclusion here is out of the question. Magruder was writing without the polite and implicit censorship of a human audience, which constantly impels us social beings to conceal some thoughts and to hide some actions. The Universal Historian, too, was strongly tempted to omit this passage from the official text, or at least to translate it into the obscurity of English, Latin, or some other dead language. Scholarship triumphed over disgust, however, and the text has not been excised in the Universal Historian's version, but the official publication is to be made available only to professional students and will have no public circulation. After quite exhausting the subject of sex, Magruder continues more acceptably:]

I have often felt close to madness, but except for the Great Delirium I have remained rational, if not fully normal in terms of a normality impossible in my circumstances. By modern (I mean, twenty-second–century) psychiatric theory, insanity is always voluntary, a willing retreat from a reality that seems unbearable. My reality is unbearable, or often seems so, and such a retreat would be a heavenly relief, but I have been unable to make it. It is tempting to drift into waking fantasy, to construct for myself images of wife and companions, but the easy way out is not for me. I talk constantly to myself, but this small concession does not evade reality: after all, I am really here to talk to! I have rigidly rejected the childish expedients of a dream world. So I remain sane, and I pay for sanity the horrible price of unmitigated loneliness.

[Here ends as much of Magruder's narrative as had been given us when the Universal Historian first handed us copies. Two slabs remain, and I shall give their contents. First, however, I wish to give an account of our next meeting at the Universal Historian's rooms. The next chapter, then, is an interlude, after which Magruder's narrative will continue to its end.]

11
Discussion with the Universal Historian

We were gathered together again, the Universal Historian, the Pragmatist, the Ethnologist, the Common Man, and I. Précieux was there, too. He had fitted in well with us and has become one of the circle of friends. We had all read Magruder's first six slabs and had come to receive copies of the last two, to follow the story to its end.

The Universal Historian had his usual crochety preliminaries: the offering of alcoholic drink, which no one now accepted, the placing of us in chairs to suit his ideas of symmetry and of protocol, the lighting of his nauseating tobacco pipe. We had little patience for the ritual that evening, but we had no choice. We were all under Magruder's spell. He seemed as real to us as if he had joined our group. There was a feeling of personal sadness that joining our group, or any other, was precisely what Magruder could not do. That was the tragedy of his story. Even before the Universal Historian was ready to take his pontifical control of the conversation, the Common Man and the Pragmatist were deep in discussion.

"I find it almost unbearably pathetic," the Common Man summed up.

"Now, I, on the contrary, find it not at all pathetic," said the Pragmatist. "To find a person pathetic is to consider him an inferior, to see in him a weaker character than your own, to assume that his misfortunes have passed you by because you are somehow more fit and worthy than he. Pathos always has a flavor of condescension. The word 'pathetic' does not fit Magruder. He is, rather, tragic. The undeserved and bravely met misfortunes of the strong are tragedy, not pathos."

"Your lecture on the nuances of words is, as usual, inadequately based on feeling for their real content," said the Universal Historian, taking charge of things in his accustomed way. "There is, of course, both pathos and tragedy in what befell Magruder, but you are making the banal error of trying to sum up in a word what was a complex, unparalleled experience undergone by an extremely intricate personality."

"I am not at all sure that I agree with any of you," the Ethnologist put in. "It seems to me that Magruder was remarkably fortunate. He was one of the luckiest men I ever heard of. I think the less of him that he did not consider the matter in that light. Instead of appreciating his luck, he went around feeling pathetic about himself."

"Do you mean you would like to have had Magruder's experience?" the Common Man asked in amazement.

"Of course I would," the Ethnologist replied, "and so would anyone with any gumption—any scientist, at least. Magruder can't have been much of a scientist. Think of his opportunities! And he muffed every one, or at best he failed to appreciate them."

"What opportunities?" asked the Pragmatist.

"You don't think it an opportunity to be the first man and the only man in the world?" the Ethnologist countered. "There Magruder was, with twenty-second–century brains and scientific training. He knew, in broad outline at least, what was to come for the next eighty million years and the principles of its historical development. He could have changed all that history, have guided it and controlled it, just because he knew and he had a human, scientific brain. Apparently this never occurred to him. All he thought of was his own survival, keeping himself sane and managing diversions from his petty personal emotions. He could have played God, and instead he only survived, for a while. He seems even to have felt pride in this ridiculous accomplishment, surviving on a level that would have seemed miserable to a twentieth-century Arawak on the upper Amazon. No. Magruder certainly was too small a man to appreciate his experience."

"I think," said the Universal Historian, "that he did come to appreciate the experience very much. The reasons for his appreciation evidently would not appeal to you. That does not mean that the reasons were not good, or that they might not demand a larger human character than succumbing to a temptation to play God—even if playing God were really possible. True understanding of Magruder's life and closer reading of his reactions and necessities would, I think, eliminate the possibility of any God-like reordering of the savage world of the Cretaceous."

"What were these reasons, then?" asked the Ethnologist. "What was Magruder's appreciation of his experience?"

"Did you ever stop to think, *really* think, what you are? And why?" the Universal Historian said.

The Ethnologist and the Pragmatist both spoke at once:

"That's two more questions, not an answer."

"Everyone knows what he is, and there are a dozen whys, of which I know four or five and a Big Brain like you knows one or two."

The Universal Historian was not perturbed either by the surliness of the Ethnologist or by the bluster of the Pragmatist.

"The questions *are* the answer," he said, "and no one has ever been in a position to think so clearly about what and why as Sam Magruder. That is what he appreciated in his experience."

"I don't get it," the Common Man said with characteristic bewilderment, at the discussion of the pedants. "Sam was a man, that's what. He wasn't any less or more a man in the Cretaceous than I am now. And he couldn't learn why any better from a live dinosaur than from the dinosaur's bones a few million years later."

"You have a point there," the Universal Historian admitted with unusual mildness—he never did quarrel as much with the Common Man as with his fellow scholars. "In your own way you may have reached the same conclusion as Magruder, but perhaps he expressed it better and with more reason."

We were by this time more than a bit bored by the quibbling discussion and anxious to get on with the last of Sam Magruder's record. Even the historian at last felt that the preliminaries were sufficient. He gave us copies of the last two slabs, as follows.

I take my time with these slabs. It gives me something else to do, and it keeps me thinking. Sidestepping a *Pentaceratops* or bashing a *Coelurosaurus* is just automatic now. One of the dinosaurs themselves could do as much. Now that I have a routine for survival, it takes no real thought. But I can try to understand, and I can write my reactions to this world. By a million-to-one shot, I might even leave them to posterity. That, at least, is something only a man could do.

I have other writing materials now. The best system is to scratch on big, flat palm leaves. I keep my calendar that way, and a sort of record of events. The events don't really matter, though, and I don't bother to transfer many of them to these stones. I write drafts of this text on palm leaves and polish them a bit before I put them on stone. Survival of an inscribed palm leaf isn't even a billion-to-one shot, but it takes a long time to write these slabs. I have been working on them for three years now and only have six done. Of course I only work on them during a couple of months in each year, and then only a few hours in each tenday.

[In the official edition there is here a note by Précieux. He comments that palm leaves are sometimes preserved as fossils in the Kirtland strata and that under his direction an energetic search has unearthed hundreds of them. There is no sign of writing on any of them. The Universal Research Foundation has decided to offer a huge reward for one of Magruder's inscribed leaves, but it looks pretty hopeless.]

"This goes mighty slow, Sam," I said to myself the other day. "You'd better be getting to the point. At best it'll be eighty million years before anyone reads this, but the writer doesn't have any eighty million years, you know."

"O.K.," I replied to myself. "So what is this point that I should be getting to?"

A few years ago, even perhaps when I started these slabs, I would not have had an answer. Now I think maybe I have.

A while back I mentioned fur in passing and did not say anything special about it. Nevertheless there is something special to say, and it has to do with the point I should be getting at.

Not long after I set up housekeeping in *Pentaceratops* Valley I began to have trouble with food storage. I stacked seeds, fruit, bulbs, and dried meat in a sort of wooden crib with slats close enough together to keep out even a small dinosaur. Yet stuff kept disappearing. I looked around carefully, and I figured it out.

"Sam," I said, "you've got mice!"

I took a deep pot and filled it half full of water. I balanced a stick on the rim and put a few seeds on the end that hung over the water. I set the whole thing up near the food crib. Next day, sure enough, there was a drowned mouse in the water. At least, it looked like a mouse and was that size, but on closer inspection I saw it was not one. Its nose was too pointy, its tail was too bushy, and it had a lot of sharp, pricking teeth but no gnawers or grinders like a mouse.

[In this version you are spared a snooty note by Saurier, who points out that Magruder should have known that rodents were not to evolve until some 20 million years later. This is substantiated by Saurier's usual pedantic assortment of data and references.]

At that time my approach to things was still, of necessity, just about 100 percent practical. Philosophy, if you want to call it that, had to wait till later. What impressed me about this critter was that it had soft, brownish fur, and that fur would be a lot warmer and more comfortable than reed or palm mats. The small size was a drawback, but it was only a matter of trapping enough and sewing skins together with a bone awl and sinew. The little devils soon got wise to my water-jar trap, but I kept a jump ahead of them in inventing new deadfalls and snares. It was not long before I had enough for three fine, warm robes. I slept between them at night and threw one over my shoulder on chilly days.

Toward the end of that project, I caught several of the little fur-bearers alive. I put a couple of them in a cage made of small branches—they weren't really rodents and couldn't gnaw their way out. They ate almost anything but seemed to prefer worms. I think I had some vague idea of raising my own fur and saving the trouble of trapping.

I remember the exact moment when a completely different idea came to me. It seems now that I should have thought of it when I saw the very first one, but you do not do much fancy thinking while you are still fighting an apparently losing battle for bare survival. The battle has not ended—yet—but after a while I was winning it. Then one day I was looking at the little beasts in the cage and listening to them squeal.

"Why, Sam!" I suddenly exclaimed. "That's your great-grandpa a few million times removed!"

That struck me as comic. I put a finger in the cage and pretended to shake hands. "Howdy, Great-grandpa!" I said. Great-grandpa nipped me, drawing a bead of blood. He wasn't yet a wise enough father to know his several-million-greats-grandson.

Think of that little devil, that tiny warm ball of fur! A mammal in the Age of Dinosaurs! A puny, insignificant little being, managing to stay alive somehow in a world that belonged to the hordes of scaly reptiles. His ancestors, I knew, had once been reptiles, too. But somewhere along the line they had developed new tricks for survival. They began to have their young alive, instead of laying eggs. Mama gave milk for the young and protected them through the period when the vast majority of reptiles die. They became warm-blooded and so could live in colder places and could be active at night, when most of the reptiles were dormant.

I'd like to go on and say that there was a triumph of brains over brawn, but I can't truthfully. Not as of the Cretaceous. The plain fact is that Great-grandpa was one of the dumbest brutes I ever met. I could no more teach him tricks, or even common docile civility, than I could tame a dinosaur. Any real advantage of intelligence lay in the future.

What a future! Insignificant now, rather unpleasant (to tell the truth), this little brute was the ancestor of the lords of the earth! His blood flows in my own veins. His descendants would inherit some spark that would keep them fighting successfully in the long struggle for survival. They would come into their own long after the great dinosaurs had failed. Is it not, indeed, that drive that animates me now? Here is the real reason for my own survival here, lost in the wilderness of time. My personal survival here is not important, to be sure. It no longer seems very important even to me. To you, reader (if by odd chance I have a reader), to you the important thing is not *my* survival but the survival of that savage little furry creature I am looking at. You, with your culture and civilization, are the outcome of his struggles and the realization of his potentialities.

Pardon the clumsy (but sincere) attempt at eloquence. I never was—will be, perhaps I mean—very good even at the composition of dry scientific papers. I really can't express my feelings of awe, of the ridiculous, and yes, almost of fear as I crouched face to face with this puny ancestor of myself and of all the rest of mankind.

I have a fair smattering of genetics and of practical animal breeding, learned in citizenship school before I specialized as a chronologist. I toyed long with the idea of selectively breeding the little mammals. I knew their tremendous possibilities, and I have no doubt I could have speeded up their evolution, perhaps by some millions of years. But for what good? They have the spark, themselves. They are going to make it. Their descendents will be men, and they'll get there under their own power. Interference from one of those same descendants, even as a boost along the way, is not necessary. It would, in fact, be sacrilege. What is holy in mankind is that mankind, through this little beast and so many others, has created itself.

["Here," said the Universal Historian when we later discussed this passage, "is where Magruder refuses to play God, and where he sees the what and why of himself, of you, and of me." "It sounds to me as if he thought that we *are* God," said the Ethnologist. "I don't think that is what he means," put in the Common Man somewhat shyly, "and I think I agree with him."]

So I opened the cage and I said, "Go with God, Great-grandpa!" and I meant it.

13

Magruder's Narrative.

Slab 8:

The End

I lost count there a little at first, but I must be over sixty years old now, counting together my two severed lives. Even without my accident, that's a ripe old age in the Cretaceous. I haven't much time left or much strength left to finish these slabs and to bury them where they'll have a chance, however slight, of being preserved—and found.

I have written mostly at *Pentaceratops* Valley, but that is not the place for the slabs. The valley is being eroded, and anything buried there must be washed out and ground to pieces in the millions of years to come. The swamp is the place. There each flood buries things deeper. The earth groans and buckles under the load—and preserves it. I am there now, near where I first saw the Cretaceous. The slabs are here. I brought the others down last year, and this year a final one, blank, for my last words. As soon as this is finished, I'll bury them deeply in the ooze.

The accident—well, it had to happen sooner or later. I suppose I've slowed down, and perhaps I've become a little careless. I've dodged so many dinosaurs. I dodged one too many and was careless once too often. The brute—it was a tyrannosaur—got me by the leg. Fortunately, you might say, he shook me loose, tearing off the leg at the knee, and he didn't see where the rest of me fell. I tied up the stump and crawled away, but I'm done. That was yesterday and I can't last much more than another day at best.

There; the first seven slabs are safe, as safe as I can manage.

There isn't much more to say. I've had no joy, but a little satisfaction, from this long ordeal. I have often wondered why I kept going. That, at least, I have learned and I know it now at the end. There could be no hope and no reward. I always recognized that bitter truth. But I am a man, and a man is responsible for himself.

["May he rest in peace," said the Common Man. For once, no one else said anything.]

Afterword

The Truth of Fiction:
An Exegesis of
G. G. Simpson's
Dinosaur Fantasy
by Stephen Jay Gould

I. Fiction's Domain in Science

If man, as Protagoras said, is the measure of all things, then all fiction must record the author's life, however cryptically—and we must honor Havelock Ellis's dictum that "every artist writes his own autobiography." George Gaylord Simpson was, physically, a small man, but his influence over my profession of paleontology can only recall Cassius's description of Caesar: "He doth bestride the narrow world like a Colossus; and we petty men walk under his huge legs, and peep about."

Science fiction has always been among the most intellectual of our literatures. Therefore, when a scientist with such a powerful mind and personality dabbles in this genre (especially for his own delectation, and not explicitly for publication), we must ask whether he has written a *roman à clef* under the guise of simple amusement—and we must scrutinize Sam Magruder for a key to George Gaylord Simpson and his troubled, brilliant psyche. Thus, in another section of commentary, Simpson's daughter Joan Burns wonders and searches. I must also do the same, for Simpson's inspiration led me into paleontology, and our ambiguous personal relationship (I do not think that Simpson knew any other mode of interaction with colleagues) shaped my career and my concerns. In addition, and primarily, I want to attempt an exegesis beyond the personal, for *Sam Magruder* is also a novel about a great profession and a major body of scientific ideas—paleontology (particularly its star subject of dinosaurs) and evolutionary theory, the keystone of all biology.

Ironically, fiction can often provide a truer and deeper account of empirical subjects than genres supposedly dedicated to factual accounting. This situation arises because many modes of nonfiction develop strong constraints and traditions that prevent (unintentionally in most cases) any approach to factual adequacy—whereas fiction, under its protective guise of storytelling, remains free to be incisive. For example, in writing a recent piece on the history of baseball biographies before the modern "kiss and tell" era, I realized that constraints of the hagiographical tradition—the need to depict each ballplayer as a moral paragon off the field and a committed, humble striver at bat—made "factual" biography a tissue of fabrication, and left truer accounts of gambling, whoring, and other shenanigans to the fictional stories of fine writers like Ring Lardner.

Factual science writing does not labor under such onerous and truth-distorting constraints, but a variety of other traditions does prevent any revelation of the full range of a scientist's ideas. In particular, the requirements for sobriety, for caution, for "sticking to inferences properly drawn from known facts," preclude the reasoned speculations, even the flights of potentially rewarding fancy, that all creative minds must employ. All good scientists operate in this abductive, hermeneutical world, but they are not allowed to write about these forms of mentality in their conventional genres. But if a scientist also has talent for fiction, then these constraints disappear—and, ironically, a truer account of the full range of scientific reasoning may actually grace a work of fiction than a sober monograph of fact.

I first became aware of this paradoxical principle when I introduced the ice-age novels of the great Finnish paleontologist Björn Kurtén—for in these books, Kurtén could conjure and speculate with wonderful insight about the real relationship of Cro-Magnon and Neanderthal people in Europe, while books on science would not allow this material because no fossil evidence of these interactions exist (though circumstantial reasoning virtually requires that rich contacts must have occurred, and the subject has been frequently treated by novelists—as by William Golding in *The Inheritors* and Jean Auel in her trilogy on the clan of the cave bear).

The Dechronization of Sam Magruder follows this fine tradition as a fictional work providing good insight into the body and soul of a profession, as well as into the psyche of an author. I therefore structure this afterword into three sections of exegesis: what Sam Magruder teaches us about (1) dinosaurs in particular; (2) evolutionary theory in general; and (3) even larger philosophies of life and how to live, as seen through the eyes of George Gaylord Simpson. And so, we move from the particular (dinosaurs) to the most general, but only through the insight of one extraordinary human being—for man is, indeed, the measure of all things.

II. Of Dinosaurs

Although Sam Magruder's own theory leads him to fall into a random spot of our geological past, Simpson contrived to make that moment a particularly interesting point in time—near the end of the era of dinosaurs. Simpson's treatment of paleontology's all-time stars tells us a great deal about the history of human attitudes, and the practices of technical study, towards these quintessential items of prehistory.

Much of the commentary consists of paleontological in-jokes and subtle sendups of professional practice—which makes me think that Simpson really did write for his own amusement (or to share with immediate colleagues), and not for publication (although, on second thought, he takes such pains to explain these parochialisms in layman's terms that perhaps he wrote for all potential purposes at once). For example, Sam Magruder almost fails to recognize his first dinosaur because his image of human restoration failed to match his ocular reality:

> Difficulty in recognition arose from the limitations of paleontological restoration. The colors of

prehistoric animals are unknown. Playing it safe, artists have not dared use the emerald-green hue of the creature I now saw before me. They show the eyes as brown or black, not the startling crimson of the reality before me. My mental image from student days was all the wrong colors. Would you immediately recognize a bright red, stripeless tiger or a purple-spotted squirrel?

(Interestingly, by modern standards, Simpson was quite conservative in his speculative choice of colors. He stuck to conventional green, though changing the hue from dull to dazzling. Contemporary iconoclasts, interpreting many of the frills, bumps and horns of dinosaurs as devices for sexual display and combat, prefer an amazing array of brightly conspicuous colors, by analogy to peacock's tails and other organs of similar function in modern animals.)

In a more dangerous misperception based on a false iconographic expectation, Magruder almost doesn't see the brilliant white teeth of an approaching tyrannosaur:

In a sort of hypnotic horror, I thought inconsequentially, "But your teeth should be dark brown!" I had seen the tyrannosaur skull in the Universal Natural History Museum, and its teeth were deeply colored. I had never stopped to think that the discoloration was the result of mineralization and that in the living animal the teeth would be white, as they are.

Particularly revealing is the effort that Simpson makes (at a length that truly does compromise the literary flow of the story) to correct a common misimpression that giant sauropod dinosaurs died out in the Jurassic and didn't survive into later Cretaceous times. (I can vouch for the common error among lay dinosaur aficionados, though all professionals know the true geological ranges. I often have to correct the same mistake among students, but the point scarcely seems crucial, unless your intent be to settle scores and clear away annoyances— for persistent minor errors of pure ignorance are galling to perfectionistic professionals, as I can attest.) So Magruder first sees a sauropod, thinks he is in the Jurassic, but then changes his mind:

> Later I saw so many species that I knew to be much later in age that I had to revise my estimate. This is certainly the late Cretaceous. . . . Evidently the sauropods survived much longer than I remember from my professional school days, or perhaps the paleontologists of 2162 have slipped up on this point.

Simpson then hammers the point home with a didactic note written by one of Magruder's interpreters in 2162 (as a clever literary device, Simpson's book consists of Magruder's narrative, preserved in tablets that he buried into Cretaceous strata, accompanied by commentary from colleagues in 2162 who found and published the tablets):

Pioneer paleontologists did, indeed, think that the sauropods became extinct soon after the late Jurassic. As early as the twentieth century it was, however, discovered that they continued into the Late Cretaceous. . . . Magruder's course in paleontology may have skipped this detail, or he may simply have forgotten it.

But most revealing is Simpson's attitude towards the great dinosaur reinterpretation of the late 1960s and 1970s—their reconceptualization from slow, lumbering, dim-witted, cold-blooded retards, doomed only for an early death as soon as sleeker mammals came along, to anatomically intricate, powerful, fast, adequately intelligent, possibly warm-blooded creatures who held little mammals at bay for 100 million years and would probably still be ruling the Earth if some unexpected and probably catastrophic cause had not precipitated their fortuitous extinction. Simpson does not quite ally himself with the true denigrators, but his expressed views are decidedly old school (as he had been trained and as he evidently felt a need to defend against the young upstarts entering his profession). The dinosaurs that Magruder meets are cold-blooded and torpid, thus providing peace and respite in the night: "Like all dinosaurs, their sluggish reptilian metabolism requires external warmth to stoke their fires. They are quiescent in the cool night air, and do not stir dangerously until the morning sun has limbered them."

Magruder describes *Triceratops* as a creature of

"grotesque awkwardness," though modern reconstructions favor a sleeker version of a limber rhino. Coelurosaurs, those smart, nimble, and agile hoppers of the new reconstructions, are incompetent in Magruder's world: "The mouth, usually foolishly agape, has small teeth or none. Their only defense is flight. They are moronic even for dinosaurs."

Most revealingly, Simpson's dinosaurs are stone dumb. Magruder escapes best by hiding after a first spotting, for the dinosaurs of his world are too stupid to remember what they had just been pursuing. Magruder describes his method for escaping a tyrannosaur. You let it run after you and leap aside at the last moment, for the awkward animal has no agility, cannot change direction quickly, and must continue to charge straight ahead. Then you hide, and the dumb beast just forgets what he had been after:

> When it finally stopped, I was hidden among the few trees still standing. It looked about aimlessly. Obviously its tiny reptilian brain had lost all memory of what the excitement was about. It wandered about for a few minutes, then loped off around the shore and out of sight. I rejoiced in being *Homo sapiens* and marked up one score for our side.

To evade a smaller carnivorous gorgosaur, Magruder climbs a tree:

> I did not move, and it finally forgot I was there and went off in search of other prey. That is one

universal trait of dinosaur psychology: they seem
to have practically no memories at all. They
never persist at anything, because they forget
what it was.

Simpson's traditionalist attitude towards dinosaurs can
also help to resolve a puzzle about the text of Sam Magruder: the date of its composition. Simpson's dyspepsia
towards the Young Turks of his field, particularly towards Bob Bakker's arguments for warm-blooded dinosaurs, largely pushed in the popular press (and also to
Simpson's immense displeasure, for this reason),
emerges in a particularly sharp passage—which can only
have been written after 1970, thereby dating the entire
manuscript (or at least this passage as an insertion):

That brings up a point that I could clear up for
the paleontologists if I could communicate with
them. In the latter part of the twentieth century
one of them [obviously Bob Bakker] had—will
have, I mean—the idea that dinosaurs might
have been warm-blooded like birds and mammals rather than cold-blooded like their closest
twentieth-century relatives, the crocodiles and
alligators. . . . Now that I am living among dinosaurs, I know that they are all cold-blooded in
the usual sense of that word—or are poikilothermal, to put it in more accurately and more
technically. The idea that they might be—have
been—warm-blooded (homoiothermal) has—
will have—a lot of publicity for a while just

because it was touted as sensational news. There really was no evidence for it, and when it ceased to be news it was quietly dropped.

On this matter, Simpson was a poor prophet by Magruder's anachronistic foresight. The issue remains much with us—as a subject of interesting debate in the professional literature.

III. Of Evolutionary Theory

George Gaylord Simpson was, unquestionably, the greatest vertebrate paleontologist of the twentieth century, perhaps the greatest of all time (or at least since Cuvier's founding days of the early nineteenth century). He was a master at the conventional form of collection and close description that forms the stock-in-trade of the profession, and he became, by early specialization, the world's leading expert on the oldest mammals that lived in the time of dinosaurs. But Simpson's status as paragon does not rest on his empirical work; others did as well in this domain. Simpson was, par excellence, a brilliant theorist who brought a conceptually backwards field of traditional paleontology into synthesis with the Neo-Darwinian consensus that solidified in the biological sciences during the 1930's. Inevitably, therefore, if *The Dechronization of Sam Magruder* be a work of autobiography in part, its text must contain interesting discussion of evolutionary theory as well, not only of dinosaur factuality.

Theoretical insight pervades the entire book, right

from the very premise in Simpson's remarkably clever device for Magruder's time travel. No subject has a greater pedigree of ingenuity in science fiction than the construction of rationales for moving either forward or backward into time, but Magruder's method—based on the deep philosophical issue, dating to Greek science, of whether the world exists as a continuous flux or a quantized series of discrete states (the nub of Zeno's arrow paradox, for example)—is wonderfully thoughtful. Magruder believes that time is quantized, as a series of points rather than a flux. But we cannot perceive the discrete nature of time because the points, like the frames of a movie, go by so fast. But Magruder is an experimentalist—and he figures out a way to slow time's flow by so many orders of magnitude that the individual dots of time and the spaces become palpable. He succeeds in his experiment, but then has the misfortune of slipping into the hole between two dots of time—right back to some random moment of the past!

The Dechronization of Sam Magruder is rich with references to issues in evolutionary theory. Since I have no space to turn this essay into a treatise on Darwinism (nor would you have the patience), let me provide two examples to give a flavor of the richness in this text. As a major accomplishment in his career, Simpson discredited a host of older paleontological theories that favored a concept of nonadaptive evolutionary "momentum" or internally driven, ineluctable trends. Earlier theorists had argued, for example, that lineages might have geological "life cycles" akin to an individual's birth, maturity, and senescence—and that, for example, a lineage might become static and cease to change as a result of racial old age. Simpson, as a firm Darwinian committed to the adaptive basis of all major evolutionary forms and patterns (a predicted consequence of evolution by natural selection), discredited the old notions of momentum by providing adaptationist interpretations for supposed examples of trends running independently of (or even contrary to) natural selection. Simpson emphasized this theme both in his popular books (*The Meaning of Evolution*) and his technical writings (*Tempo and Mode in Evolution*).

On his second Cretaceous day, Sam Magruder escapes a dinosaur only to be nearly eaten by a crocodile (he does lose a finger to the beast). Ever thinking, even in this worst adversity, Sam is struck by the similarity of this Cretaceous crocodile to the contemporary versions he has seen in zoos. He then engages in a remarkable soliloquy, contrasting the old momentum theories with his Darwinian conviction that crocodiles have been stable as a result of excellent adaptation in an unchanging environment. Finally, he offers the ultimate Darwinian explanation for human success— not an inherent trend of our innate superiority (as the old anti-Darwinian theorists might have argued), but the good fortune of our ancestors' lives in a challenging and changing environment that required continual evolutionary activity:

> It was a crocodile. . . . It looked, as far as I could see, exactly like crocodiles in zoos in 2162 A.D.

There is a successful adaptation for you! ... It has been said by some theorists that cases like that of the crocodile, virtually unchanged for 100 million years and more, represent a failure of the evolutionary force, a blind alley, or a long senescence. As I gazed at my antagonist, it occurred to me how false this is. Here was no failure but an adaptation so successful, so perfect that once developed it never needed to change. Is it, perhaps, not the success but the failure of adaptation that has forced evolving life onward to what we, at least, consider higher levels? The crocodile in his sluggish waters had perfectly mastered life in an unchanging environment. No challenge arose. Our ancestors lived in a more evanescent world, where what was adaptation at one time became an inadaptive burden in 100,000, 1,000,000, or 10 million years. For them, their adaptation was always a blind struggle to keep up, to face new conditions, to exploit new opportunities.

As a second example, Simpson became very interested, late in his career, in the nature of historical science as the study and explanation of unique and complex events, rather than the repeated predictability of simpler phenomena produced by the actions of unchanging physical laws. (He referred to such historical vs. predictable phenomena as "configurational" and "immanent" respectively.) In one of his most famous articles, entitled

"On the Non-Prevalence of Humanoids," Simpson argued that if intelligent life existed elsewhere in the universe, it could not resemble us in appearance, for we have been shaped by a contingent series of evolutionary events so rich in their number, and so unrepeatable in their intricacy, that the same sequence could never occur again in the same way—not even on this planet if we could start all over again from the first single-celled living form. Humanoids, in other words, are not predictable consequences of nature's laws, but fortuitous results of history's contingency on this particular planet. Sam Magruder acknowledges this theme when he contemplates his tablets near the end of his Cretaceous life and exclaims: "For reading, art, and music, I have only what I myself create. These slabs are at present the only reading matter on earth, probably all there is in the universe."

IV. Of Broader Philosophy Through Simpson's Individual Eyes

Anyone who knew George Gaylord Simpson would recognize his particular interests, pleasures, and concerns in the text of *Sam Magruder*. For example, Simpson loved languages and was quite a polyglot in his own accomplishments. Many of his characters are parodies in the languages he knew—the terrible German theorist von Schrechlich, the French geologist Pierre Précieux ("Precious Stone"), and the Russian institute director Kto Znayet ("Who Knows"). In what we might anachronistically view today as a multiculturalist paean, his future world does not use English for its international tongue, but Interlingual Swahili (for Simpson knew that Swahili, a Bantu language with substantial Arabic intermixture, had an indigenous African core but also served as a *lingua franca* with roots in African commerce—hence the Arabic inputs).

Simpson also loved to drink and smoke; I never saw him relaxed or happy without these accouterments, usually both. The text, at a length that I found uncomfortable and with attempted humor that, to my reading, doesn't work, discourses in detail about the anachronistic smoking and drinking of the major narrator in 2162 (most of his contemporaries follow the more modern practice of swallowing inebrione pills).

But these are only the superficial signs of Simpson's presence in the text. George Gaylord Simpson left his mark on Sam Magruder in a much deeper way, by basing the story upon his most profound fears. I don't want to sound like a two-bit Freudian quack, but *Sam Magruder* is a stunning text largely because Simpson threw open a window into his own *Angst*, both the petty parts and the profound.

I knew Simpson during the last fifteen years of his life, when he was the most honored and the most revered paleontologist in the world. Yet I never encountered a man so apparently lonely (save for the comfort of immediate family), so dissatisfied, so craving for recognition, yet so incapable of satisfaction. I wanted to shake him (or hug him, if he would have permitted either)—and tell him how much we all loved him, how his work had been our chief joy and inspiration. But no one could find a middle ground to please him. One either spoke truly and therefore had, at least on occasion, to express some disagreement with something he had once said—and this he could not bear. Or else one played the toady and agreed with everything he said—and this he could bear even less, for his fierce intellectual honesty could not tolerate false ingratiation. And so, one of the world's most honored scientists wallowed in a miasma of doubt and anger, always fearing that future generations would ignore him and that all his work would ultimately go for naught.

These themes of loneliness and fear of intellectual impotence (not being heard, remembered, believed, or honored) pervade the text and story line of *Sam Magruder* and elevate the work from an instructive fable about the earth's past to a profound work about the sense and meaning of human life. In this sense, and I think without question, Sam Magruder is George Gaylord Simpson—and Magruder's one-way life sentence in a Cretaceous prison represents much of Simpson's take on his own existence. (I even played some cabalistic games to see if the name Samuel Magruder might be some sort of code for Simpson, George Gaylord—but I got nowhere.)

Consider the stunning opening image of Simpson's novella—as good as anything Sartre, or any of the French existentialist writers, ever composed on the ineluctability of being alone and responsible for one's actions. A group of colleagues, bearing the titles of their

status, are engaged in what appears to be a purely theoretical discussion:

> "What would you do," asked the Universal His-
> torian, "what could you do if you knew you were
> going to be utterly alone for the rest of your
> life?"
>
> "That's something we'll never find out," said
> the Pragmatist. "The situation could not arise."

The Ethnologist then proposes Tibetan anchorites, immured in their caves, and the Common Man speaks of
castaways on desert islands. But they all agree that neither case truly qualifies—for the anchorite must be fed,
and could pass a note to his suppliers saying "Get me
out of here"; while the castaway lives in hope, however
slim, of eventual rescue. They all finally agree that no
one can be utterly alone with no conceivable hope of
contact—and then the Historian springs the story of Sam
Magruder!

So Sam Magruder—because he must—invents and
hones his skills in the arts of survival he never learned
in his urban world (and he develops quite credible ca-
pacity in all manner of achievements from fire making,
to weaponry, to charting of seasons and food sources).
But, because Magruder is Simpson, he is tortured by the
impossibility of immediate recognition and by the near
certainty that no person will ever honor his accomplishments (for he knows that future discovery of his buried
slabs is a million-to-one shot, though it does come
to pass, and he can't derive any pleasure from future

findings in any case). What a strikingly exaggerated image of Simpson's own deepest fears in his real life! Magruder writes of his slabs:

> There is a chance in a million that someone will read this someday. I will never know, however, and here I have learned that benefiting mankind is at the same time a social and a selfish occupation. It is no good unless you see the benefit and get some sort of approval for it.

Magruder does take some pleasure in being right, even if he cannot enjoy the recognition of others. His falling into the past, as a bitter example, does prove his quantum theory of time: "Not that it will do me or anyone the slightest good to know that I disappeared by dechronization. It does, at least, prove my theory. I try to get from that such bitter satisfaction as I can."

Most of all, however (and in line with Simpson's personal fears that his own knowledge would have no influence), Magruder is frustrated that he has learned so little from being the only person with direct experience of dinosaurs. He cannot help future paleontologists at all. He has learned nothing about reasons for forthcoming extinction of the dinosaurs, and he can scarcely add a thing, even to the anatomical descriptions:

> In short, I know no more about the causes for their disappearance than if I had never seen one.... What can I say that will help the paleontologist of the future, if any should chance to

see this record? Little or nothing, really, beyond
confirmation of the cold-bloodedness of the dinosaurs. . . . At least, I do know their colors.

But then, just as we begin to fear that Simpson's novella
will end in the narrowness of his own bitterness and
paranoia, the great, warm, and expansive humanist in
him—the saving grace that always shone forth in his
writing to conquer his personal misery—takes over and
rescues Sam Magruder with a touch of universality.

Near the end, after they have read six of Magruder's
eight slabs, the Universal Historian meets again with his
colleagues—and they have a moral argument about Magruder's worthiness. Was he a pathetic man who flunked
the most golden opportunity ever provided to a scientist,
and who not only learned so little but didn't even try to
influence future time while residing in the past? The
Ethnologist is most negative:

> Magruder can't have been much of a scientist.
> Think of his opportunities! And he muffed
> every one, or at best he failed to appreciate
> them. . . . There Magruder was, with twenty-
> second-century brains and scientific training. He
> knew, in broad outline at least, what was to
> come for the next eighty million years and the
> principles of historical development. He could
> have changed all that history, have guided it and
> controlled it, just because he knew and he had
> a human, scientific brain. Apparently this never
> occurred to him. All he thought of was his own

survival, keeping himself sane and managing diversions from his petty personal emotions.

But the Universal Historian defends Magruder as both profound and compassionate. He responds to the Ethnologist:

> I think . . . that he did come to appreciate the experience very much. The reasons for his appreciation evidently would not appeal to you. That does not mean that the reasons were not good, or that they might not demand a larger human character than succumbing to a temptation to play God—even if playing God were really possible.

On the seventh slab, Magruder's own testimony upholds the Universal Historian, and clinches the novella. Remember that the great theme of time travel into the past has always been, and almost must be, the power to alter futures—leading, of course, to the paradox that the present from which one entered the past should not exist after the alteration. The film trilogy of *Back to the Future* represents the most influential recent example in popular culture. Even when the flow of the past conquers an individual's power to alter time—as in the remarkably original and inventive, and much underrated, film *Groundhog Day*—the central theme remains: how can an individual, entering the past with knowledge of an actually realized future, influence that future by impacting this new go-round of the past?

In this context, and given this firm tradition, Sam Magruder does something truly heroic—thus elevating his novella into literature. After feeling so impotent for so many years, after learning so little and impacting his world so lightly, Magruder finds a potential way to play God with the earth's future. He sets a trap for animals that are raiding his food stores—and catches small mammals close to our own ancestry. He keeps them in a cage. He starts to think and realizes that he could wield significant planetary power:

> I have a fair smattering of genetics and of practical animal breeding, learned in citizenship school before I specialized as a chronologist. I toyed long with the idea of selectively breeding the little mammals. I knew their tremendous possibilities, and I have no doubt I could have speeded up their evolution, perhaps by some millions of years.

But he desists, for reasoned morality, and not from lassitude, indecision, or cynicism:

> But for what good? They have the spark, themselves. They are going to make it. Their descendants will be men, and they'll get there under their own power. Interference from one of those same descendants, even as a boost along the way, is not necessary. It would, in fact, be sacrilege. What is holy in mankind is that mankind, through this little beast and so many

others, has created itself. . . . So I opened the cage and I said, "Go with God, Great-grandpa!" and I meant it.

George Gaylord Simpson was, by professional training, the world's expert on mammals of this era. His Magruder may not have learned much about dinosaurs, but he understood the little mammals in the biggest way. He let time alone and snatched hope from the jaws of despair. He then personalized the lesson for his own lonely, yet heroic, life—and he found adequate peace (which may be all an honest man can expect) as he scratched his dying words into the last slab:

> I've had no joy, but a little satisfaction, from this long ordeal. I have often wondered why I kept going. That, at least, I have learned and I know it now at the end. There could be no hope and no reward. I always recognized that bitter truth. But I am a man, and a man is responsible for himself.

A Memoir

by Joan Simpson Burns

Magruder might well have disappeared forever when my stepmother, Anne Roe, died a few years after G. G. Simpson's death. Now that she was gone too, only a few files remained at the retirement community in Tucson, Arizona, where she had lived during her last years. No one seemed interested in these. The bulk of my father's papers had already gone to the American Philosophical Society.

Sitting at Anne's desk—she had used an alcove of her apartment as a small office—I was struck by how little remained of the mountains of material Anne and George had accumulated during their lifetimes. It had been an enormous project to send on to libraries and archives everything she and their lawyer had considered of scientific importance or historical interest. As executor of both estates, Richard Duffield had taken all of the additional papers he needed to do his job. My sisters, Helen Vishniac and Elizabeth Simpson Wurr, not inclined to collect things in any case, had gone through the apartment and were ready to relegate remainders to the trash. I opted to take anything not wanted by the others as part of my division of the property. I asked myself why *The Dechronization of Sam Magruder* had not found a home.

Everything left was shipped to my home in Massachusetts. This simple act, moving the leftovers away from the site of mourning and into a new home, brought them a new life. I had not thought of this when I sent them; I was just driven to do so. Now, looking on the same things without the terrible presence of the recent dead, I began to understand their value. The same thing had happened when GG's sister passed away. She was a remarkable painter, trained in the cultural hotbed of Paris in the 1920s, and many of her paintings had found their way to me in the same manner, as remainders. With new frames they quickly drew the astonished attention of my sisters and comments from artists and art dealers who visited my home.

The question remained: in the system which organized all of my parents' belongings, what had been the place of *Magruder*? It had been kept, just as had so much connected with GGS from childhood on, but obviously kept apart from his serious works and papers. If they had not taken it seriously, why had my parents kept it at all? Now I finally sat down to read the story through. Immediately I was struck by its unusual double quality. It revealed much about the character of the extraordinary scientist who wrote it, and it was a good read.

I thought, "This ought to be published, and in a way that will allow the reader to see both the biographical and chronographical sides of the story." To accomplish this, some commentary would have to be added. The problem, of course, was to find writers who knew both about the genre of science fiction and the particular science of paleontology. Indeed, the overlap between science and fiction has been, since Edgar Allan Poe, increasingly important in our culture, and I wanted something said about how *Magruder* fit into that trend. Arthur C. Clarke came immediately to mind. I wrote and told him my plan, and invited him to introduce this small book. To my delight, he agreed.

In addition to a steady diet of academic works, GGS consumed detective stories and science fiction each night before he went to sleep. Apparently while still a teenager he had briefly entertained the idea of being a writer but, after that ambition gave way to the ones he eventually fulfilled, I do not believe he continued to read other kinds of fiction. From my own youth, I remember that he would sit by himself on Christmas day and read the latest *Oz* book. These he brought as presents to Washington, D.C., where I lived with my grandparents. Amongst the fiction he did read, GG was particularly interested in the works of Arthur C. Clarke, Isaac Asimov, and Dorothy Sayers, and that is why I was especially pleased to have Clarke's input.

Most of GG's writing was devoted to studying the history of life on earth. This becomes the subject matter of fiction in *Magruder*, and I wanted the reader to have some support on this side as well. Again, it was easy to think of the right person. You will recognize Stephen Jay Gould as the contemporary author most capable of bringing science to life. I knew, as well, that he had been a student of my father's. When I received his response to my letter, saying that he would be pleased to help put the novella in its context, I felt confident that I had built a proper home for *Magruder*.

One may wonder why an enormously successful scientist like George Gaylord Simpson would write science fiction. In addition to his academic writings, he had written a number of books which were, at the height of his career in the postwar decades, very popular. In books such as *The Meaning of Evolution* and *This View of Life*, he permitted himself not only scientific description and theory but also speculation about the meaning of science and its discoveries. Too, his works sometimes were explicitly autobiographical, recounting his travels in whole (*Attending Marvels: A Patagonian Journal*) or in part (*Penguins*) or his life as he saw it (*Concession to the Improbable*). So a need to make known his life and philosophy was probably not the main force behind the writing of *Magruder*. Then what was?

Perhaps it simply amused him to write the novella, although he might have been disconcerted by how much of his personality he unconsciously reveals in it. I am quite sure he felt he could do anything, could have been anything, including a successful writer of fiction. His only other substantial piece of fiction, written with my stepmother, was a murder mystery called *Trouble in the*

Tropics. Perhaps he thought these brief forays into the world of fiction could make him some money. Indeed, he reminded his family not infrequently that he had stayed in a comparatively unremunerative field (science) when he could have made his fortune if he had chosen a career in finance. Family legend has it that, while quite young, he had briefly been a runner at the Chicago Stock Exchange.

It is easy to identify him with Magruder in certain ways. There was his propensity for travel and his great interest and expertise in biogeography. Travel was hard for him (*viz* Sam Magruder) but compelling (again, *viz* Sam Magruder). He remained disappointed all of his life that he never succeeded in entering Mongolia. Like Magruder, in the course of his travels his leg was badly damaged. There are kinds of self-expression which come through in *Magruder* and not in any other of the more than six hundred works he published during his lifetime.

The central strand in the story is Magruder's isolation. Like many highly successful men, my father limited his acknowledgment of the extent to which he had depended on other people. For instance, George Whitaker, his laboratory and field assistant for many of his pre-Harvard years at the American Museum of Natural History, who saved his life when he was nearly destroyed by an accident in the upper reaches of the Amazon. Also, my grandfather, who taught him from an early age just how extraordinary he was. The unfaltering admiration of two females, his wife, Anne Roe, and his sister, Martha Simpson Eastlake, was throughout his life a crucial personal prop. There are certain empty spaces in *Magruder* in this respect.

Splendid Isolation was the title of one of his books, but isolation has another side to it. Loaded though he was with honors, GGS still felt himself quite alone. His biographer, Léo F. Laporte, points to anomie as a component of his personality. I think that is not quite right. I do believe he felt himself different from but more capable than others, as indeed Magruder is. There are also hints that in his later years he wondered about the future of his work; indeed, it was the new thinking of Stephen Jay Gould and others that induced this uncertainty. *The Dechronization of Sam Magruder* deals with the idea of enormous discoveries that other men, in the future, may never realize have occurred. Magruder uncovers them anyway and attempts as best he can to pass them on, as did GGS.

Despite the noblest efforts of this sort, Magruder and Simpson could not but have worried that it was all for nothing. The largest ambitions, precisely because they pretend to reach so far and change so much, always bring the greatest fears. This, I think, is the best explanation for *Magruder*. It is a fiction which expresses fears about the durability of work and accomplishment and life itself. In other works my father took up the Meaning of Life. In *Magruder* he holds a mirror up before the Scientist of Life, to consider the meaning of that particular life . . . his own. This is something most of us never have the courage to do at all. GGS found that strength in fiction.

Acknowledgments

First and foremost, Stephen Jay Gould and Arthur C. Clarke are thanked for their invaluable contributions to this small volume.

Professor Gould's continuing optimism about the project was remarkable. I trust he knows the depth of my appreciation.

There has been much luck involved, not the least of which was my discovery that an editor with whom I had worked at Harcourt Brace, William B. Goodman, was now an author's agent. His collaboration with Russell Galen, the agent who has been instrumental in arranging publication, does credit to both of them, and I am grateful for their support and encouragement. Much credit also goes to Robert Weil, senior editor at St. Martin's Press, who was immediately attracted to the Magruder story. I thank him for his contagious enthusiasm.

G. G. Simpson's biographer, Léo F. Laporte, has been extraordinarily kind and helpful.

Special thanks goes to one of Simpson's grandsons who is, as it happens, my son. Peter Alexander Meyers, busy with his own work as a political theorist, contributed beyond measure.

And there is Frank Winslow Smith.

—JOAN SIMPSON BURNS
High Mowing
July 1995

About the Authors

GEORGE GAYLORD SIMPSON (1902–1984) was a fine linguist, a prolific writer, and a brilliant biologist. His participation with others on the modern synthetic theory of evolution was widely regarded as originative. He was the recipient of numerous honorary degrees and awards (including the National Medal of Science), both in the United States and abroad. He was a fellow of the American Philosophical Society, the National Academy of Science, and Great Britain's Royal Society. After many years in New York at the Museum of Natural History and Columbia University, he was appointed to a professorship at Harvard University in 1959. At the same time his wife, Anne Roe, herself a distinguished psychologist, was also so honored, making them the first married couple with full professorships at that university.

During World War II, Simpson served in Intelligence

with the Army in North Africa, Sicily, and Italy, where he gained notoriety when he respectfully refused to comply with General George Patton's order to remove his "pink whiskers." He reminded the General that an officer was permitted to maintain a beard with his Commanding Officer's consent so long as it was kept neatly trimmed. *His* Commanding Officer was General Eisenhower.

ARTHUR C. CLARKE is one of the most highly regarded science fiction writers of all time. Among his many classic works of fiction and nonfiction are *Childhood's End, Rendezvous with Rama, 2001: A Space Odyssey,* and *The Fountains of Paradise.* Born in Somerset, England, in 1917, he has resided in Sri Lanka since 1956.

STEPHEN JAY GOULD, Alexander Agassiz Professor of Zoology in the Museum of Comparative Zoology at Harvard University and Frederick P. Rose Honorary Curator in Invertebrates at the American Museum of Natural History, teaches biology, geology, and the history of science at Harvard. He is the author, among other books, of *Time's Arrow, Time's Cycle: Myth and Metaphor in the Discovery of Geolitic Time, Bully for the Brontosaurus,* and *Dinosaur in a Haystack.*

JOAN SIMPSON BURNS is an author and editor living now in Williamstown, Massachusetts. She has published a number of books, including *Dinosaur Hunt* (with George Whitaker) and *The Awkward Embrace,* a study of cultural institutions and their managers. George Gaylord Simpson was her father.

A Note About the Dinosaur Names Used in This Book

Many species of dinosaurs are known by several names. When newly discovered dinosaur remains are described in a scientific journal by a paleontologist, the animal is given a name by the describer. Later, it is sometimes found that these remains match those of another dinosaur discovered and described earlier. In such a case, the earlier name has precedence, and the later name is subsumed under the older. Two of the names for the dinosaurs illustrated in this book, *Gorgosaurus* and *Coelosaurus*, have now been rendered obsolete, though they were in use when Simpson wrote his book. In order to maintain consistency with the text, the older names have been used in the captions. Today, these theropod dinosaurs are known respectively as *Albertosaurus* and *Struthiomimus*.